55737

FIC Clarke, Richard
Cla The copperdust hills

DATE			

9402124

YANKTON COMMUNITY LIBRARY
YANKTON, SOUTH DAKOTA

© THE BAKER & TAYLOR CO.

THE COPPERDUST HILLS

Other titles in the Walker Western series:
THE GUNS OF MORGETTE, G.G. Boyer
FRONTIER STEEL, Nevada Carter
THE SCARLET HILLS, Harry Beck
THE FORTUNE FINDERS, Jacquin Sanders
RANGE TROUBLE, Clay Allen
THE LOCKHART BREED, T.V. Olsen
SMASH THE WILD BUNCH, Giles A. Lutz
THE APPALOOSA, Robert MacLeod
TEXAS FEVER, Donald Hamilton
BANNON'S LAW, Lauran Paine

For further information write to:
Walker Westerns, Walker & Co.,
720 Fifth Avenue, New York, NY 10019

THE COPPERDUST HILLS

Richard Clarke

WALKER AND COMPANY
NEW YORK

Copyright © 1983 by Richard Clarke

All rights reserved. No part of this book may be reproduced or transmitted in any form or by any means, electric or mechanical, including photocopying, recording, or by any information storage and retrieval system, without permission in writing from the Publisher.

All the characters and events portrayed in this story are fictitious.

First published in the United States of America in 1983 by the Walker Publishing Company, Inc.

Published simultaneously in Canada by John Wiley & Sons Canada, Limited, Rexdale, Ontario.

ISBN: 0-8027-4018-9

Library of Congress Catalog Card Number: 82-51230

Printed in the United States of America

10 9 8 7 6 5 4 3 2 1

CHAPTER 1

Brothers

THE sun was high, and a huge distant valley was pale green in morning brilliance. Where the pair of horsemen had crossed ice-field peaks, there was eye-hurting glare and dangerous patches of black ice that even horses shod with caulks could cross only by maintaining perfect balance.

The mountains were high enough so that their rims had been ice fields for eons. Until the pair of riders got below timberline, above which there was no growth except scrub brush in rock crevices, the footing had been poor. Centuries of run-off snow water, constantly changing course, had carried the soil away, down to bedrock.

At timberline they had encountered better footing for their saddle animals; five miles down the cordillera, they were in timber—mostly black-barked, mighty fir trees whose spiky tops formed an almost impenetrable barrier to sunlight, except occasionally where slanting shafts lent the hushed, brooding forest a cathedral effect.

Mark Forrest poked his head up out of the thick collar of an old blanket-coat and looked back. Thirty feet ahead on a downhill game trail, his brother also looked back, his beard-stubbled, half-frozen face showing awe, and said, "You and your damned shortcuts."

Mark straightened in the saddle, gazing ahead. "We made it, didn't we?" He gestured with a gloved hand. "Look down yonder. That's one hell of a big valley, and the sun's shining." His pale eyes crinkled. "Where's your spirit of adventure, John?"

The answer came back curtly. "It's froze, like all the rest of me. Mark, I'll bet you no one's crossed those damned mountains in the springtime before, unless it was In'ians." As he said this, John Forrest cautiously unbuttoned his sheep-pelt coat and blew out a big breath to see if it still steamed. "I was scairt pea green up there. It was worse'n riding over glass—and if anything happened, hell, our clothes would of been out of style before anyone found us."

They were in their thirties, rangy men with bony, wide shoulders, deep chests, and rugged, tough-set features. Mark was three years older than John, but there was no way to tell that from looking at them.

They were rangemen. They had worked the ranges of Montana, Wyoming, and Colorado. Once they had teamed up to operate a freighting business over in Idaho, and Mark had tooled coaches for the Inland Stage & Freight Company down through Ratón Pass. That was the year John had married. Seven months later, he became a widower.

They had decided, after the worst of the Wyoming winter was past, that they'd both had enough of cold country, and had headed southward. Mark had been in northern New Mexico. John never had and was impressed with what Mark had said about the warm climate—warm most of the time, anyway—and the opportunities down there for tophand range riders. But crossing the stair-stepped hundred-mile mass of mountains had not been what John had anticipated; and even when they were far enough downslope to be able to tie their coats behind their cantles, loosen their collars, and gradually relax as that bone-chilling cold was left behind, John twisted once in a while to gaze back. They had successfully crossed snowpacks and ice fields no human being in his right mind would have considered crossing, especially this early in the year.

The timbered mountainsides were shadowy to ride through, but there was warmth closer to the lower elevations, and that made all the difference for both men and animals. A man might suffer back up there, but a horse carrying a man suffered more. The Forrest brothers were lifelong stockmen; they cared for their mounts, rode only good ones, and favored them every chance they got.

That was what had motivated them to seek a place to night-camp while still on the mountainside, even though that huge green valley looked tantalizingly close by mid-afternoon. The horses had been without decent feed since the day before.

There were glades—called parks in the northern high country—scattered throughout the lower mountains. They had probably been created by lightning-started fires generations earlier; to exhausted horses and tired men, they were miniature paradises.

Some of those parks were several hundred acres in size, with creeks running through them, stirrup-high grass, blue sky directly above, and they appeared unexpectedly in the middle of thousands of acres of black-barked fir trees.

Generally, these clearings were not very large, perhaps twenty to forty acres in size. The one John led his brother out into was even smaller, no more than ten acres of grass and sunshine and blue sky. There were probably better ones around, but John did not look for them. He rode out midway, saw the creek through waist-high pale grass, swung to the ground, flexed stiff knees, and looked around to where Mark was sitting up and gazing around.

"Good enough," John said. He knelt to hobble his big bay horse with the intelligent, calm dark eyes. "It's flat. I never before been in a country where both ways is uphill."

Mark dismounted wordlessly, pitched his bedroll and big saddlebags to the ground, loosened his cincha, gave his seal brown, thoroughbred-looking horse a fond pat, and dropped to one knee to set the hobbles before unsaddling. "You'll like it," he said. "A man could do a lot worse than settle down here. Maybe scrape together a few sections of land and get some cows."

John was lifting down his saddle when he replied to that. "I've had a taste of settling down. There's only one way to do it, and if a man can't do it that way, he's better off to keep riding."

Mark said nothing. He did not even glance up. His brother's grief was less now than it had been, but it was still there. Mark had never been married, had never really been in love, but he could sense what John had gone through. He thought his brother would probably never entirely forget the woman he had loved, married, and had watched die when an epidemic had struck. John knew three things very well: cattle, horses, and men. His knowledge of men gave him the wisdom not to speak just now.

They made their meager camp and watched the horses pick at grass-heads, standing in strong feed to their shoulders. They scraped out a place for their cooking fire, brought water from the creek for boiling dry jerky and making coffee, then lay back with sunlight baking out the last vestiges of that congealing cold they had had to endure since reaching the northward rims.

Neither of them had shaved in days. Their hair was too long and their clothes needed scrubbing, but these were things they had been tolerating as conditions of their trade for many years. They would take care of them when the time came; until it came, they would ignore them.

John leaned the booted saddlegun against his upended saddle and said, "There's game in these mountains, and I sure as hell could do with something besides jerky stew."

Mark lay full-length in warm grass, hat over his face. "Lots of bear sign, some deer sign but not very much, and cougars. But my guess is that we'll eat fish. These creeks are bound to have 'em." He lifted the hat slightly to see what his brother was doing, dropped it back down, and spoke again. "Did you see barefoot horse tracks where we turned off to come into this meadow?"

"Yeah. Some cow outfit down yonder probably lost 'em. Or maybe something spooked 'em. Otherwise I can't imagine why loose stock would come up into the mountains. Not where there's cougar and bear scent."

Mark sighed with deep pleasure as sunlight beat directly down upon him. "Maybe. What I was thinkin' is that if someone had a remuda up this close to the mountains, there must be a ranch not too far off."

John was shaving jerky into a little tin pot using a wicked-bladed Barlow knife. "No need to hurry and get work," he told his brother. "I'd as soon loaf for a week or two." He shot a sidelong, accusing glance in Mark's direction, which Mark did not see. "After what we came through, I could use some time recovering."

There was the faint sound of a dry snort from beneath the hat. "Ma babied you too much, John."

The big Barlow knife hung poised in the air. "Babied me? The hell she did! But even if she did, that's better'n havin' my brother darn near get me frozen to death and scairt out of five years of my life riding over glass-rock and black ice."

For a while Mark was silent, his chest rising and falling in deep, even sweeps. "All right, we'll loaf. Fact is, right this minute I'd favor lying in the sun, doing not a damned thing for a while."

"And if we get riding jobs, all we'll get for it is money," John said.

Again the black hat that hid Mark Forrest's face remained motionless for a while before he spoke. "Yeah. Money. Which reminds me—I got nine dollars left; how about you?"

"Sixteen. Trouble with you, Mark, is that you waste money."

The black hat lifted, and a pair of pale gray eyes turned toward the scraped place where John was filling the little pot with water over the shaved jerky to make their supper.

"Waste it!" exclaimed the elder brother. "Hell, I never wasted money in my life. You want to know why? Because I never had that much. I saw some wild onions back yonder about where we rode out here. They'd put flavor into that stew."

"You're not makin' it."

Mark sighed and sank back down in the grass again. "If I'd stayed with the Flatiron outfit," he said in a voice muffled by the hat over his face, "I wouldn't be here now waiting to eat jerky stew with no flavor to it."

"If you'd stayed with the Flatiron," replied John, "you'd have had to have married that widow woman who owned the outfit, and jerky stew without wild onions would be a lot better."

"How do you know?" asked Mark.

"I worked there, too, you know. She had her eye on you from the first, an' she was big enough to eat hay and mean enough to punch you out of the saddle."

Mark was silent so long his brother thought he had fallen asleep, then his muffled voice said, "You remember Otis Ludlow?"

John smiled. "Yeah. If ever a man was not fit to be a range boss, it was Otis. Why she kept him on as her foreman I can't figure."

The voice from beneath the hat said drily, "No, you probably can't. But someday, when I figure you're old enough to know about such things, I'll tell you."

John's wide shoulders reared back as he turned to regard the sprawled, lanky shape of his brother. He said, "Naw, I don't believe it."

"It's a fact, John."

"How do you know it's a fact?"

The muffled voice came slowly this time. "Once, when I was down in the brakes choosin' out some of those damned savvy horses they had at Flatiron. . . . I didn't see the buggy until later, but there they were in among the creek willows like a pair of a bear cubs mauling and grunting."

"I don't believe it. Really? Her and Otis Ludlow?"

"For a damned gospel fact. I slipped away from there as fast as I could, left half the damned horses in the willow brakes and took the rest of 'em to the yard and corralled 'em."

For a moment John sat gazing at the little pile of twigs he had gathered to make their supper fire with; then he suddenly broke into laughter.

A couple of yards away Mark sat up, dumped the hat carelessly on the back of his head, and joined in the laughter.

CHAPTER 2

Downslope

THEY remained camped in the meadow for three days, longer than they had stopped over at any other camp since they had struck out.

There were fish in the creek, as Mark had predicted, but they were as skittish as colts; just a hint of a shadow over the water sent them scurrying. Nonetheless Mark and John caught some of the plumpest rainbows and browns they had ever seen, fried them crisp, and lingered over some of the best eating a rangeman can experience.

They hunted, too, but had no luck, even though they found a fair amount of deer sign. What they found more of answered the question about why venison was so rare in this area: bear sign, and lots of it.

They had a brush with a bear on the evening of the third day after they had dressed their fish at creekside, and a shambling old sow came upwind, sniffing for fish entrails. First she spooked the horses, which alerted Mark and John to her coming. Then she reared up out of the grass about a hundred yards south of the camp, and although the grass was waist-high to a man, it struck her below the belly. She had a little age on her, as indicated by the white over her weak little eyes. Her nose and ears were scarred, and, standing erect, she was about seven feet tall. She probably weighed close to twelve hundred pounds.

Her fur was acquiring a gloss, but she had not completely

shed off yet. As Mark studied her, he guessed she was wormy; most of them were because, by and large, they lived off carrion.

He did not move. Neither did his brother, who had got up to his feet with a saddlegun in one fist when the horses had taken fright. The sow-bear could not see them very well at that distance. Like all of her kind, she did not have good eyesight, but she could detect a sound farther away than most other animals and had a very keen sense of smell; if by chance this old girl also had a cub or two somewhere around, she could be very disagreeable.

For a while the big sow swung her head from side to side, wrinkling her nose. When she figured out where the man-scent was coming from, she dropped back down on all fours and stood utterly still, peering in the direction of the camp.

It was a long wait for the two men. The bear, to whom time meant nothing, was perfectly willing to make all her ponderous judgments before moving. Mark whispered. "I wish to hell the hobbles were off the horses."

John whispered back. "If she turns toward the horses across the meadow, I'll drop her." But she finally resumed her shambling, pigeon-toed walk up the creek bank as hunger won out.

In fact, she was less than sixty yards from the watching men when she found where the fish had been cleaned, and she began eating. She certainly knew there were two-legged creatures somewhere close by; their scent was not only on the wind, it was also along the watercourse. She ate heartily, occasionally looking around without so much as changing the cadence of her chewing. When she had cleaned up the last remnant, she turned with what might have been monumental disdain and went shambling back southward again.

Mark shifted stance, shoved back his hat, and watched. She also had to know now that there were horses around, which meant that unless she made a decent kill shortly, she might return for a horsemeat feast about sundown or later. "I suppose," he told his brother, "we should have killed the old girl."

John was leaning aside the Winchester when he replied, "Naw; if a man shot everything that bothered him, there wouldn't be much left."

Mark turned to resume his place in the pressed-flat grass of their camp. "You rested?" he asked, watching his brother remove damp grass from the fish they would have for supper.

"Yeah. You want to head down into that valley?"

"Might as well. We got to put new shoes on the horses, and if there's a town down there somewhere, we might get shorn and sluiced off."

"And find a saloon. I'm still cold."

Mark laughed.

After supper, they brought the horses closer to camp and stoked up the fire. They kept it stoked up even though one or the other had to interrupt his slumber and raise up out of a bedroll to pitch in the wood. Bears feared fire above anything. It was no guarantee that the old bear would not return, but it would slow her down if she did.

By dawn she had not come back to the little meadow. Mark was frying the last of their fish when John rolled out, heading for the creek to wash. It was cold. Mornings were always cold in the high mountains.

The horses were full as dug-in ticks; each man had to let out his billets just to snug up the cinches. When they were loaded and ready to ride, Mark struck out in the lead, as sunlight appeared over the treetops. It hit the riders squarely in the face; they tipped down floppy hatbrims.

There was no game. They got back out through the trees to the place where they had left shod-horse prints turning westerly into the little park, and Mark reined downhill.

There were not even any birds evident for two hours, until it had warmed up enough to encourage them to venture forth. Then they entered the private domain of a particularly evil-tempered camp-robber, who scolded them unmercifully, following them across his area, flitting from treetop to treetop as he kept up his raucous and ringing denunciations.

They were only a couple of miles uphill above the vast green valley when they halted to noon the horses and lie in fragrant warmth for an hour or so. Mark was gingerly trying to pick enough blackcap berries to make a mouthful, from a flourishing thicket that had ten barbed thorns for each berry, when the horses abruptly snorted and began backing clear of something below in the tall grass. Mark's brown gelding was facing whatever was directly in front of him hidden in grass stalks, little ears rigidly pointing, head low, nostrils distended to snort. He was not terrified, or he would have spun and fled, but he was backing away in a determined manner.

John turned, picking up the Winchester as he moved toward their mounts. Behind him, Mark, who had not removed the saddlegun from the boot under his saddle fender, walked out, pulling loose the buckskin thong that held his Colt in its hip holster.

Mark's horse gave a sudden bound, rising and whirling on its rear legs. The Forrest brothers saw the short, fat, greeny, ropelike body of a timber rattler whip in the air. The snake had his fangs in the horse's left foreleg.

The horse came down, pawing violently, and the snake fell clear. Mark went after the bitten horse while John hurried to the place where the snake had landed. The rattler was whipping away, but something, probably the pound of booted feet coming up onto him, made the wrist-thick snake, most deadly of rattlers, stop and coil.

John picked up a round boulder, poised it high, and

dropped it onto the snake. The rattler tried to strike; the big stone broke his back and punched him an inch into mouldy earth. It was still thrashing and hissing and rattling when John turned back. When the heat left the day, the rattler would stop writhing and die.

Mark had already cut two slits in the horse's foreleg, one crossways through the pair of fang marks, the other vertically between them, and was kneading the flesh to squeeze out as much bloody venom as he could. He looked up and said, "Hold his head, John."

John caught hold of the reins and cheekpiece and said, "He was a big one."

"Did you kill him?"

"Yeah. That's a hell of a bite."

Mark did not speak, but continued to work with the punctured upper leg until there was sweat on his shirt front. The horse was shivering, his nostrils flared and his eyes glassy. Fear and shock were uppermost now, but within another few minutes the poison would start working. They led the horse back to where they had halted, to remove the outfit from his back. He limped badly, more from the impromptu surgery than from the bite. When they had done everything for him they could do, Mark and John hunkered in speckled and fragrant tree shade, somberly watching. When the poison took effect, the horse would be very sick. There was no snake west of the Missouri River more deadly than a timber rattler.

Mark wagged his head, settled to the ground while rolling a smoke, and softly said, "I wish that son of a bitch had tried to bite me instead."

John said nothing because there was nothing to be said. A man and the horse he had been riding for several years were always close, and a really good horse, like Mark's gelding, meant even more to his rider.

It was warm up where they hunkered. Down across that

big valley, it was downright hot; they could see heat waves out there. The horse hung in place, his head near the ground, his body dark with sweat. Mark found a creek and carried water back. The horse would not drink, so he used it to wash the animal's back.

John remained by the upended saddle. When his brother walked back, John said, "He'll likely make it, Mark. But he's not goin' to carry anyone on his back for a spell. Tell you what I think we ought to do — he's not even goin' to feel like bein' led for a few days, so you stay up here with him, and I'll go scout down out through the foothills across the valley and find a place where I can get a horse to fetch back up here for you. If I find a town, I'll fetch back some grub, and we can spend a week or so here until your horse can travel."

Mark rolled and lit a smoke, keeping his face averted in the direction of the horse. "Yeah. We don't need another horse as much as we'll need some grub. I didn't see any sign of a town out there, though. You might have to find a ranch."

John rose. "I'll find something." He paused a moment, gazing at the deathly ill horse, then said, "Gawddamn snakes anyway," and went over to his own horse to ride away.

Left alone with his sick mount, Mark continued to fetch cool water to help hold down the fever; but as the sun shifted, he desisted because he did not want his horse wet after sundown.

With little else to do, Mark made a survey of the area, seeking more rattlers. He found none, but somewhere out among the big trees he picked up a bushy-tailed tree squirrel that followed him back to his camp, visible only when the man suddenly whirled to catch a glimpse before the squirrel ducked out of sight on the far side of a tree.

Some crows came up to roost along toward evening,

evidently having spent the pleasantly warm day out over the big valley. They were astonished to find a two-legged creature up there with a horse, and after letting go with several unmusical loud squawks, sprang off their treetops to beat a disorderly and raffish retreat.

CHAPTER 3

The Foothills

MARK would not have bet money that his seal brown gelding would be alive come sunup, but it was—barely, though, and flat out on his side, full of fever and venom. He did not respond when his owner brought more creek water to try to hold the fever down as the day turned warm.

Fortunately, the horse had been in good shape, better shape in fact than most horses were; he had never been allowed to put on wet-weight, and he was young—seven years old—but these factors Mark Forrest recognized as only marginally in his favor. They would make the difference between living and dying if it came down to things like that tipping the balance.

The horse sweated profusely, which had a dehydrating effect, but he was never lucid long enough to drink; after a while Mark abandoned the effort to try and get water down him.

He spent the day alternately nursing his horse and exploring the immediate area, where he found more of those week-old barefoot horse tracks, to which he paid no attention. He also found a salt lick about a hundred yards east of his camp. It had layers of animal tracks roundabout, and Mother Nature had providentially established a little seepage spring no more than a half mile from the lick. There he also found a grassless area of hardpan where generations of game animals had packed the earth until it rang like iron.

Once, through an opening among the black-barked trees, he saw several horsemen loping southward as though they might have been up in the lower foothills. They were too far away to hear a shout, and he was too well-camouflaged by tree shade for them to see him wave his hat, even if they had turned to look back, which they did not do.

On his walk back to the horse, he speculated about those horsemen. They had clearly been rangemen, which probably meant there was a cow outfit not too far distant. Perhaps his brother had found the ranch by now, although he had seen no sign of a solitary rider heading northward.

The horse was shivering again and covered with sweat. If there was any improvement in his condition, Mark did not notice it as he set about making a thin flame to cook jerky stew by.

The evening was warm. Mark thought that was simply the result of day-long heat; but later, when the scimitar moon was up in its star-studded setting and there should have been at least a hint of coolness, the warmth remained.

Mark did not dwell upon this unusual condition for long. If he had, he would probably have decided from long experience that the warm night meant a wet-front was moving in, and that within a day or two it would rain.

He went over to shove his coat under the horse's head because the animal was beginning to beat his head upon the ground. Then he squatted and had his after-dinner smoke, thinking about horses and snakes and a number of other things until the horse stopped beating his head. Then Mark went back to his blankets and rolled in. John would show up in the morning; it was not critical whether he showed up today or tomorrow anyway, since Mark was not going anywhere and still had enough jerky for a few more stews.

By sunup of the following day, the horse was feebly trying

to lift his head, so Mark went after more water, and this time when he propped the horse's head against his leg, the animal drank both the stewpot and his owner's hat empty. Then he was content to lie back again until Mark returned with more water.

He was as weak as a kitten, but, horselike, he wanted to stand. Mark had to force him back several times in order to prevent him from lunging, then falling and perhaps injuring himself. He talked to the horse, reasoned with him, scolded him, even laughed at him a little, mostly because he was so relieved that there was at last a glimmer of sound hope. But not many horses had a sense of humor, and ill horses had none at all, so the contest continued, the eleven-hundred-pound horse having to yield—probably for the first time in his life—to the less-than-two-hundred-pound man.

By midday the horse was no longer slipping off into periods of stupor, and by mid-afternoon he could drink all the water Mark brought back in both the little stewpot and his hat. Also by mid-afternoon, the horse was stubbornly committed to the idea that he could get up onto all four feet.

Mark still flopped him back and sat on his neck. The horse accepted this; but the moment Mark rose, the horse would try again. His owner finally told him he was the most pig-headed big damned fool he had ever known, then stood by while the horse lunged. Mark lunged with him, leaning all his weight on the offside. The horse got up, legs sprung wide apart, body quivering, his head held low, eyes blinking rapidly as dizziness came.

It was a full hour before Mark felt the horse could stand without aid, and he eased away slightly. The horse did not go down, but straining had brought a rush of blood out of the swollen shoulder, so Mark went back to dig out his only remaining clean shirt to make a bandage.

That evening Mark had no time to speculate about the continued absence of his brother. He was far too occupied with his horse; while the animal was clearly on the mend, he was still too feeble to do more than lurch and stumble toward the nearest grass clumps, and Mark had to remain out there with him. The horse was also completely vulnerable to predators, which by now had surely picked up his scent, along with the odor of blood accompanying it.

Some large predator did arrive in the vicinity toward full dark. Mark heard it, listened to it padding in a cautious surround. He thought it was probably a cougar, but he never saw the animal; perhaps because the human scent was strong, too, whatever was out there eventually departed.

Mark did not get back to his blankets until the warm night was well advanced, and then finally he sniffed, scanned as much of the sky as was visible up through stiff fir-tops, and recognized a more substantial proof than the warmth; the stars were milkily shrouded, and the moon had huge, diaphanous vapor rings around it. It was going to rain.

He made a final trip out to the horse, satisfied himself that if it fell there were no jagged stumps or exposed sharp rocks close enough to cause injury, talked quietly to the animal for a while, then went back and bedded down. He was tired. Acting as nurse to an uncooperative eleven-hundred-pound patient was enough to wear out the most durable man on earth.

He awaked with the sun rising out over the huge valley, as it sent peripheral shafts of dusty brilliance up through the trees. He looked over and saw the horse lying down with his legs folded under him like a big dog. Evidently the horse had fallen in the night and had elected not to try to get back up again. When Mark gazed over there, moving to sit up in his blankets, the seal-brown cast a surly, sullen look upon him, and Mark grinned.

"Next time, you big idiot, don't wait until the son-of-a-bitch gets coiled."

The horse continued to stare at the man stonily.

Today Mark Forrest had time to consider things other than his horse. He ate jerky stew, helped the horse stand again, helped it shamble over to where there were grass shoots, then left and walked eastward out where the forest was thinnest and stood upon an exposed old lichen-covered rock, studying the vast open country southward.

There was no sign of a horseman out there. There was no sign of any kind of life until he'd been keeping his vigil for about an hour, when a band of horses appeared out of the east. They scuffed dust as they traveled at an easy lope. Then, without apparent reason, they stopped, looked all around, and dropped their heads to crop grass. They made Mark smile; they were acting as though they were mustangs, and every one of them was a broken stock horse complete with the little telltale spots of white hair on his withers, the result of saddle sores, which in turn were the result of incorrect saddling and filthy saddle blankets. Cowboys, an old man had once told Mark Forrest over in Idaho, were never good horsemen, and very few were even fair cowmen.

He went back to see what the horse was up to. He had managed to graze feebly around an area of perhaps six or eight yards, and swung his head to look around at the approaching man with a hint of his former quiet curiosity. Mark talked to him; the horse dropped his head and resumed eating. As far as he was concerned, appetite came first; it always came first with horses.

Mark went over to the spindly creek, stripped, and had an allover bath, confident that when he got back his brother would be there—perhaps even with some tinned peaches, the best treat a rangeman could imagine.

Not only was John not at the camp, but when Mark hiked back to the rock outcropping to scan the seemingly endless flat miles of range country, there still was no sign of him. Even those horses were gone.

He sat down and rolled a smoke, scanning the immense valley carefully, blocking in sections of it and patiently waiting for movement. There was none, neither up close nor at a great distance.

He smoked and thought and finally killed the cigarette, stood up, and walked slowly back to the camp. The horse was moving when the man saw him. He was weak, but he was able, which was a small miracle in itself. Perhaps it indicated that being in perfect health and being young had made the difference after all.

Throughout the warm afternoon, the horse built up additional strength and continued to try to satisfy a ravenous appetite. The man alternated between staying where he could keep an eye on the horse and going to where he could look out over the big, completely empty valley.

Eventually, with dusk mantling the valley and curtailing visibility, Mark returned to his camp and sat in silence, watching his recuperating horse and puzzling over the continued absence of his brother.

When night arrived, he made the last of the jerky into a nourishing, spicy stew, then cleaned the pot in the grass and generally got ready to strike his camp. When he had everything packed, he used his lasso-rope to snake the saddle, with its laden saddlebags, up into a tree. The only thing left was the bedroll, and later, as he rolled into it, he was not particularly worried about it falling victim to salt-starved rodents and other varmints; human smell struck pure terror into the brains of all wild animals. He would simply pitch it up as high as he could and let it hang there.

About the horse he was of two minds, but before dropping off he decided to take the animal with him. He had to; the seal-brown might be able to walk a little, to graze along, but he would never be able to elude the spring of a horsemeat-loving mountain lion or outrun a bear.

It was not a happy prospect, but then the Forrest brothers had not enjoyed very many of those in any case; they functioned as did most professional rangemen, expecting adversity of some kind most of the time, and putting up with it.

He slept until about two in the morning, when a bear came grumpily in from the west, whining and growling to himself, clearly unaware there was a man anywhere nearby; otherwise he would not have been making all that noise.

Mark sat up, reached for his six-gun, and when he heard his horse snort, rolled out and tugged his boots on, then went irritably over near the quaking horse and waited. The bear crashed through underbrush, bitterly complaining about something, then abruptly halted. He had picked up two intermingling scents, one of a horse, one of a man. All the disagreeableness vanished. He was not fearful; bears had no reason to fear any other living animal, except one, and they were not always afraid of him. This one had been in a bad mood before he reached the campsite. He was not visible, but Mark knew approximately where he was when he had halted to rear up on his hind legs and sniff, his massive, flat-to-sloping broad head swinging slightly from side to side.

Visibility was very poor. Mark had had enough encounters with bears to respect them, and an irritable bear was the most unpredictable beast on earth. He waited, the shaking horse at his side.

After a while the bear gave a loud, almost whistling grunt. Occasionally this signified fright; more often it merely signified surprise, but quite often it also meant the bear was willing to charge. If it had been daylight and Mark could have seen how the bear moved, he would know which course the beast might take, but it was dark and he had no intention of waiting until the bear charged.

Mark raised the Colt, aimed it about where he thought the bear was, and fired. Across the thunderous echo came another snorting grunt, this time of unmistakable surprise. The bear turned and went lumbering at high speed back the way he had come. The horse would have fled in the opposite direction if he had been able.

Mark let the gun hang at his side as he listened. The bear was charging through thickets with the sound of a herd of stampeding cattle. He did not even slow down.

Mark turned, talked his way up to the horse, and stroked it until most of the animal's fear diminished. Then he shoved the gun into his waistband and rolled a smoke.

It was still warm. He was wide awake. "Hell," he said, "we might as well head out now instead of waiting for sunup. It's going to take you forever just to travel a mile or two."

It did not take long to stow the bedroll and rig out the horse with his bridle. The horse, feeble though he was, seemed more eager than the man leading him among the trees to leave the campsite behind.

They went slowly, partly because the weak horse could go no faster and partly because they could not go fast in the darkness of the forest.

Mark had been right. They did not reach the last fringe of forest before the false dawn was bringing a faint brightness to the world; did not get past the last tier of trees into the grassed-over low, rolling foothills until the sun was rising; and did not get down another half to three-quarters of a mile before a great orange ball shot up over the eastern horizon and balanced upon a spiky series of cliffs miles away, sending forth molten sunlight, as dazzling as a forest fire, in all directions.

Mark halted to let the horse drink at a little warm-water creek, then allowed him a short while to rest and graze before starting forward again, down through the low slots where those rolling foothills spread east and west.

There were soiled banks of clouds in the east. If they continued to advance southward and westward, they would eventually catch the sun on its curve and bring shadows. That prospect, and the strong possibility of rainfall if it did happen, did not bother Mark Forrest as he walked along leading the weak horse, pausing now and then to retie the bandage and pat the animal.

He had no idea where he was or where he was going. Eventually, regardless of how lost a man might be, if he continued to move he would find something: a town, a ranch, or a cow camp.

He came close to the end of the foothills before the sun had climbed much. When the horse hung in the bridle, he dropped the reins so the horse could eat and strode ahead alone for a view from the last foothills. He rounded a little hill, entered a small valley with a longer and slightly higher land-swell dead ahead, and came upon a very fresh mound of earth. The dimensions were exactly right for the thought that came into his mind. He was gazing at a fresh grave.

For a short while, he was too surprised to move. Then he went closer. The earth was still crumbly underfoot; whoever had been buried here had gone into the ground no more than a few days before. There was no marker, not even a piece of wood driven into the ground.

There were shod-horse tracks around the entire area. They seemed to have come into this place from the southeast, but Mark was not sure of that and felt no inclination to backtrack to be sure.

Nearby, where a solitary old gnarled oak tree stood, a

patch of paleness reflected early sunlight. Mark walked over there; there were the unmistakable gouges made in a lower limb where a rope had sawed through soft oak bark. Turning very slowly, Mark looked back at the mound. *Someone had been hanged here, then buried!*

For a while he stood in one place looking all around—at the ground, at the grave, at the telltale lynch-marks—and finally he walked back to his horse, picked up the reins, quartered back and forth until he found what he sought— his brother's shod-horse marks coming down out of the mountains. They had been made by caulked shoes. He followed them down into the vicinity of those other, caulkless horseshoes and saw where they had been covered as the men whose horses had been wearing plates swarmed up. After that there was no additional sign of caulk marks until he led his horse away from the grave site out around that long, low land-swell to the south.

There he found the tracks again, this time intermingled with the caulkless shoes, all of them heading southward at high speed, as evinced by the way the horses had dug in each time their hooves had struck the ground.

He stopped for a long time, then went back to the grave for a closer look, and discovered something he had overlooked before. Someone had laboriously scratched two words into the soil with his boot toe—Scar Hand.

Mark knelt and reread that uneven message, made sure he was not imagining things, then arose and turned again to look at the fresh grave. A distant dark object caught his eye. He walked over to the bank of a narrow, shallow erosion gully. What had been visible from a distance was the upper part of a saddle. Standing above, looking down into the gully, he saw the whole saddle, and he recognized it. He knew that saddle as well as he knew his own rig; *it belonged to his brother.*

CHAPTER 4

Blythe

THE town of Blythe had been established by traders about a generation earlier, and it had been founded at the kind of site traders preferred when they had in mind erecting something permanent. There had to be a year-round creek, plenty of good grass, and good visibility in all directions.

The road, like the wagons and stages that now traversed it, had come later, generally following the two main trails — one coming down to Blythe from the north, the other coming up from the south — that had been the threadlike lifeline of Blythe when there were only three log buildings. Now, one of those functional log structures housed the Blythe Mercantile Company, the only large general store for a hundred miles in any direction. The second of those old log structures was now the rooming house, and the third log building was now exactly what it had been years earlier, the *calabozo:* the jailhouse.

Other buildings had been built over the years. The stage company had put up an office out in front of a large, palisaded corral. Diagonally opposite this building was Bud Arlo's saloon. There were additional places of business such as the saddle and harness shop, the combination wagon works and smithy, Jasper Tobin's livery barn — with public corrals out back — and George Franklin's gunsmithy.

Blythe was functional. It served cattle and mining interests throughout a vast area, but it was also an attractive place, with huge old cottonwood trees among the residences behind town on both sides of the main roadway, and patches of cultivated green where townsfolk had squash, potato, and corn gardens.

There were, as Bud Arlo had often said over his bar, worse places to live. Blythe flourished; when there were economic strictures elsewhere, Blythe did not suffer. Because it was isolated enough not to receive news promptly, usually by the time someone received a newspaper from beyond the Copperdust Hills telling of hard times, they had come and gone before the people of Blythe heard about them.

Bull-necked, oaken-fisted Constable Frank Hadley had echoed Bud Arlo's sentiments about the town, but with one qualifying statement. "When the riding season is on, a man don't know from one Saturday night to the next one what damn foolishness the range riders will come up with."

But Blythe was a tolerant place, mostly because it had to be; two-thirds of its prosperity derived from the big cow outfits throughout Copperdust Valley. It also helped that, as the result of a bad shootout a decade earlier, the ranchers cooperated with the Blythe Town Council. While this had not eliminated trouble, it certainly made cowboys think twice about hoorawing the town when they knew that a complaint from Constable Hadley could get them fired.

Hank Bostwick, the stage company's local superintendent, who was as large and thick and ruggedly capable as Constable Hadley, once summed it up succinctly for the council back when he had been a member: "We got a good balance. The cowmen cooperate, or they get cut off. And if you gents with stores in town think this'll ruin business, let me tell you something—it'll be a damned sight harder on the ranchers because then they'll have to get their supplies elsewhere, hauled in by freighters, which will make goods cost them three times as much and come a lot slower."

Whether the big cow outfits knew this, or whether they

simply did not want their men causing trouble in town, what Hank had called a "good balance" had been working now for over ten years and, in fact, the day the southbound stage raised dust in the roadway as it made its big swing up through the wide gateway of the corral yard Hank and Constable Hadley were discussing how much better things were in general, as compared to what they had been like back a few years. It was a pleasant day, warm and still with a faint high overcast as though it might rain in a day or two. They were loafing in the stage company office, sharing a pot of black java between them.

Carl Bronson, who had just brought in the upcountry stage, walked in from the yard, nodded around, helped himself to what remained of the coffee, put his whip in the wall rack, and sat down as he shucked off his gloves, tipped back his hat, and smiled. "You fellers got the best jobs in the whole damned territory," he said, and tasted the coffee. Carl was a large, bluff, hearty man with a drooping dragoon moustache and small, perpetually squinted pale eyes. As he punched the gloves into coat pockets, he also said, "Brought in an extra passenger, Hank. I came out of the pass, down maybe three miles, and there this feller was, sittin' on the cutbank at the side of the road. No horse, no bedroll, just sittin' there. I stopped because I thought he might be sick. He asked where I was going, I said Blythe, he handed me a silver dollar for fare, climbed in without another word, and just now got down and walked out of the yard the same way—without even noddin' his head for me stoppin' to pick him up."

Bostwick rattled the pot, found it empty, and replaced it atop the office wood stove. "Maybe he was sick, Carl. Maybe . . . where was he sitting?"

"About three miles south of the pass, at the lower end of the foothills," replied the coach driver. "Naw, he wasn't sick, but somethin' sure as hell is bothering him. I was goin' to ask where his horse and outfit was, but he walked past and climbed into the stage. He didn't want to talk, that was plain enough, and I wasn't goin' to make him do it." Bronson stood up to place the empty cup aside. "Well, hell, if I'm goin' on south, I'd better get out there. They'll have the fresh horses hitched by now." He smiled broadly. "Constable, see you day after tomorrow when I come back up through. Hank, mind your bald spot, it's goin' to rain."

After the big bluff stager had departed, Constable Hadley shifted in his chair to glance out through the solitary front window where he could see the roadway for quite a distance. From the desk, Hank Bostwick said, "I've had that happen, and felt the same way."

Frank turned. "Had what happen?"

"Get bucked off in the middle of nowhere and have to walk to a roadway to hitch a ride into town, so damn disgusted I didn't want to talk."

Frank sighed and rose from the chair with an effort. "Yeah, I guess we all have," he said, went to the door, and stood in the opening completely filling it with his big, powerful body. "How come Bronson's taking the coach on the south run, too?"

"Short-handed," replied the other man from behind his desk. "One driver quit, and two are down with the grippe, or something anyway. Hank can do it. He's about the best driver the company's got."

Constable Hadley went out to stand briefly in the shade of the overhang before crossing the wide roadway. He was on his way to Arlo's bar but got intercepted out front by Jasper Tobin, the balding, paunchy, raffish liveryman from the south end of town. Jasper had a joke to tell that he had just heard from one of the traveling harness salesmen who passed through each spring and autumn.

By the time Frank Hadley reached the bar where Bud Arlo was vigorously rubbing his bartop, the last of Bud's midday customers were gone and the only patron of the place was a solitary, faded-looking rangeman sitting by himself in a shadowy corner looking at the wall and not moving, not even touching the shot glass he had filled from the whiskey bottle on the table in front of him.

Frank Hadley saw the stranger, slid a glance over him, then stepped to the bar to relay the joke Jasper had just told him. Bud listened, then laughed and pitched aside the bar rag as he pumped two glasses of beer. Bud had a personal rule: he never drank anything stronger than beer, which he made himself in a shed across the back alley, but he would drink that any time of the day or night.

Bud was a round-faced, agreeable man in his fifties. He was a good listener and never talked about himself. Broad-shouldered and heavier than he should have been, he was slightly less than average height. At one time he'd been a cavalryman.

He jerked a thumb and lowered his voice to speak. "I'll never get rich off him. He come in, asked for a glass an' bottle, took 'em over there, set 'em up, filled the glass, then just sat there starin' at the wall."

Frank turned slowly for a second look at the nondescript range rider. "You know him?"

"Never saw him before in my life. Well, I heard a couple of Hank's drivers are down sick."

Frank nodded, turning forward again, and leaned down to get comfortable as he reached for his glass of beer. "There's always somethin' goin' around this time of year." He tasted the beer, grimaced, then frowned at Bud Arlo. "What the hell did you put in this batch—coal oil?"

Bud's eyes widened. "Coal oil? That's one of the best batches I've brewed all year. Frank, you're just not used to high-class beer is all."

Hadley tried it again and puckered his face. "If that's the best, Bud, I may go back to just plain whiskey." He put down a coin beside the two-thirds-full glass and straightened up just as the man in the gloomy far corner rose without a word and walked out of the saloon.

Bud muttered, went after the bottle and glass, picked up the silver coin the stranger had left on the table, and returned to the bar, where he poured the contents of the shot glass back into the bottle with a shake of his head.

"What in hell did he take the bottle for if he didn't figure to drink?"

"Sometimes a man's got too much on his mind." Frank said. "He acts natural but he don't think natural. That feller looked to me like someone with something bothering the hell out of him."

Bud Arlo dismissed the stranger with a gesture and a comment. "They come and they go. Some are as crazy as a pet 'coon, and some aren't."

Five minutes later Constable Hadley walked forth into the sunshine, eyed the heavens with their diaphanous prerainfall veil, then sighed and looked elsewhere. That stranger who had been inside a few minutes ago was walking toward the livery barn at the lower end of town. A handsome top-buggy with yellow running gear and bright red wheels came whipping along from the north end of town and veered in front of the general store. A pretty woman alighted, along with a dumpy older man who looked as though he probably had not smiled more than twenty times in his life.

Constable Hadley recognized the man, but not the woman. The man was Chet Small, who owned probably more range land in Copperdust Valley than any other cowman, and for a fact he didn't smile. Not that Chet Small was a disagreeable man; he was just one of those people who had little in his life to make him smile. He was a wealthy man, and the Small Ranch was not his only interest. Generally, he was well liked in Blythe and across the huge expanse of cow country. Constable Hadley had spoken to Chet Small perhaps ten times in the last ten years, and he neither liked nor disliked the man. Hadley had occasion to feel that way about several of the big ranchers with whom he had conversed no more often than he had with Chet Small. He was far more familiar with the range bosses, the foremen of the large cow ranches. They were the individuals Frank Hadley knew on a man-to-man basis.

As for the pretty woman with Chet Small, Frank was sure he had not seen her before. Chet was not married, so unless he had changed that condition recently, the pretty woman was not his wife.

Of course, there was another possibility—an intriguing one at that—but Frank did not dwell upon it. For one thing, he didn't really care what the relationship was between the handsome woman and Chet Small. For another thing, while he had been standing out there looking around, someone with a light rig had cut away from town on the west side, driving northwesterly in the direction of the distant foothills.

What held Frank Hadley's interest in the rig—obviously one of the outfits Jasper hired out down at the livery barn; they all had yellow wheels—was a shovel handle sticking up out of the whip socket.

CHAPTER 5

A Corpse

IT rained that night, not hard but steadily, beginning about eight o'clock and dwindling to an overcast mist at sunrise.

It was the kind of a rainfall stockmen liked because there was no runoff, no waste water; every drop soaked into the ground to keep the grass strong, there was no wind with the downpour, and by mid-morning the sun was clear again. If stockmen had their way, it would rain like that every two weeks all summer long; but townsmen, with muddy pathways and roads to contend with, or leaky roofs and muddy drinking water, fatalistically accepted the inevitable rainfall without feeling any enthusiasm about it at all.

Frank Hadley fired up the little potbellied stove in his jailhouse office to dry the place out; one bad feature about old log walls was that they absorbed moisture and retained it.

The clerk at the general store had told Frank that the way to cope with the clamminess was to oil the outside log walls every autumn, and while Frank had thought at the time that the suggestion made good sense, he had never mentioned it at a meeting of the town council because he knew they would agree to purchase the oil if Frank would agree to apply it.

He had breakfast and went over to the mercantile company for his mail. He then put the coffeepot atop the stove in the jailhouse office and got comfortable at the desk while reading a letter from a woman in Indiana who thought her missing husband might be in the Copperdust Hills country. She gave a description that would have fit the first fifty men Frank would encounter today when he left the office.

The other two letters contained wanted dodgers, one of a bank robber who had recently raided a bank in Denver, the other of a man calling himself Ace Dugan, who had stolen horses throughout the Rabbit Ear Pass territory of Colorado. Frank filed both dodgers in a big wooden crate in the storeroom where he had been filing posters for ten years, then went back to the front office to see if the coffee was hot.

Three men barged in out of the roadway: two youngish men, weathered and sinewy and taller than the rather dumpy, slack-faced balding man in front of them. Frank had seen the dumpy man yesterday with a handsome woman over at the general store. He pleasantly nodded and motioned toward chairs as he said, "Good morning, gents, Mr. Small." He gestured toward a string of tin cups hanging by nails on the back wall. "Fresh coffee, if you'd care for some."

Chet Small's nondescript, flaccid features did not change. His small, lusterless eyes followed Constable Hadley to his chair. The cowman spoke.

"Someone killed my range boss yesterday, Constable."

Frank's looseness slowly faded. "Howard Beasely?"

Small nodded. The pair of cowboys behind him remained impassively stationary. Gazing steadily at the surprised lawman, Chet Small said, "His horse came to the home place about suppertime last evening. The men did not find him until this morning. I have them putting him in the icehouse over behind the mercantile store. We'll eventually bury him at the ranch, but I don't want to do that until we've found his killer."

Frank said, "Where was he killed?"

"South of the foothills, I think, although he might have been killed elsewhere and packed down where they found him."

"How was he killed, Mr. Small?"

"Shot."

"In the back?"

"No, he was shot at close range in front."

"And his weapon?"

One of the lanky cowboys leaned and dropped a six-gun atop the desk. It was an old weapon with no blueing left, but it was sound enough. Frank opened the gate and slowly turned the cylinder. There were five unfired cartridges and one empty brass casing.

Frank looked up. "He got off a shot, Mr. Small."

"Possibly," agreed the wealthy cowman. "Possibly, too, the man who killed Howard fired off a round to make it seem as though Howard got off a shot."

Frank put the gun aside and studied the three bitter-faced men opposite him. "Why? What would be the reason?"

Chet Small's answer was brusque. "What matters, Constable, is that whoever killed Howard Beasely was on my land, trespassing. He had no right to be there. Maybe Howard ordered him off, and the man shot Howard, but whether Howard got off a shot or not, the man who killed him was violating the law when he shot Howard."

It was not the kind of a reason most men would use to send the law after someone, but it was the kind of a reason someone like Chet Small would use to justify running down and executing someone. He wanted a killer caught; any reason would be sufficient.

Frank stood up and went to the stove to fill a cup, then to face his visitors as he said, "Any landmarks up there where it happened?"

Chet Small gave his meager, quick nod again. "We drove a stake in the ground and tied a red bandana to it. If you head due northwest from town, keeping the topmost rim of the northward mountains dead in front, you'll find the stake. When will you be going out there, Constable?"

"As soon as I finish my coffee, Mr. Small."

Without another word, Chet Small led his riders out of the office. The last man closed the door gently.

Frank's coffee tasted acid. He put the cup atop the woodbox and went to stand by his desk, gazing at Howard Beasely's Colt.

He had known the foreman for about eight years, ever since Beasely had hired on with Chet Small. They had never been close friends—their interests were too different—but they had been friendly, had shared a few drinks over Bud's bar, had swapped a few traveling-salemen stories, and had negotiated a few times when riders from the Small Ranch had hoorawed the town.

Howard had been a dedicated ranch foreman, as loyal to his brand as most rangemen were. He was a no-nonsense individual; Frank had heard a few disgruntled riders complain that Beasely drove his riding crew too hard, but that was not an uncommon complaint.

Frank did not know for a fact that Howard Beasely was a good man with a gun or his fists, but he had logically assumed that he was; a range boss for a place as large as the Small Ranch was rarely otherwise.

But somebody had been better with a gun, evidently.

Frank finished the coffee, got his hat, and hiked down through the dog-trot between the mercantile building and the adjoining structure to the north, emerged in the back alley on the east side of town, and approached the icehouse with its massive, sawdust-filled two-foot-thick walls.

At the risk of having the general store proprietor yell profanities at him, Frank left the icehouse door open. There were no windows, and with the door closed it was not only bitterly cold in there; it was also eerily dark.

Howard Beasely had been wrapped in a soiled piece of wagon-bow canvas. Frank removed it and recognized Howard by his scarred right hand, which had shiny, discolored skin that looked as tight as a drumhead across the back of it. Then he leaned farther and recognized the face.

The killing had indeed taken place at close range; there were singed places and powder burns on the clothing as well as around the puckery little bluish hole in Howard's chest where the slug had struck him squarely through the middle of his brisket. Death had been instantaneous.

But there were other marks, too. Frank shifted knees before leaning to examine the body more closely. Small's range boss had been in a fight. From the bruises and marks on his face, and also on his knuckles, it must have been quite a battle.

Beasely had been one of those spare, stringy men without an ounce of fat on him anywhere—the durable, rawhide-tough kind. But, while that was all to the good when a man got into difficulties, what helped as much, or maybe even more, was the ability to brawl well. The longer Frank Hadley hunkered there on one knee with icehouse cold getting into his bones, the more it began to appear to him that the other man had been the best of the two of them. Howard had taken a hard beating before they had gotten down to guns.

Frank went back outside, closed the door, and stood awhile waiting for the cold to depart. Then he returned slowly and thoughtfully to the jailhouse, picked up his jacket, his booted Winchester, and went down the back alley to the livery barn for his horse. He probably would not be missed until evening; perhaps not even then, since this was a Tuesday, not a Saturday.

He had plenty of time, provided he did not waste any getting up there. It was a long ride, but not an unpleasant one this time of year.

He picked up buggy tracks, speculated they might have been made by the rig he had seen yesterday afternoon with the shovel sticking up out of the whip socket, and did not pay much attention to them for a couple of miles, until it became clear that the tracks were heading in the same direction Frank was heading.

After another few miles, he ran into something even more interesting. There was another set of buggy-tire impressions in the rain-moistened ground, fresher than the first set, perhaps made no later than early this morning. They headed back southward in the direction of town.

The buggy driver seemed to have driven north, then, much later, to have come back south. Frank rolled and smoked a cigarette, thinking that when he got back to town he'd go down to Jasper Tobin's barn and find out who'd hired that rig yesterday.

He found the stake with the bandana wrapped around it, but that was all he did find up there, just below the foremost stretch of foothill country. If there had been any significant signs, the rain had obliterated them. There were shod-horse marks that seemed to have come in from the west to this place. And there were buggy tracks passing directly through the area where the killing had taken place, but both were rain-washed until there was nothing distinctive about any of them.

For a while Frank led his horse out and around, studying the land with increasing frustration. If he could have searched up here before the rainfall, he was confident he would have found something. Now, as he led his horse back to the stake, then mounted, about all he knew that he had not known before was that the person who had been driving that buggy had crossed through here, and might or might not have seen or heard anything.

Anyone traveling up toward the foothills with a shovel in his rig was more than likely a prospector. There were always a few men turning earth or panning the mountain streams for a sign of color this time of year, after the winter storms had passed and any flake gold near the surface might have been washed to the lower elevations.

He considered the foothills, thought of exploring up there, then eyed the slant of the sun and turned back in the direction of town. It would be dark by the time he got back as it was.

He had passed along perhaps two miles when he saw two men sitting like Indians, watching him. They were off on his right, perhaps a mile distant. He was not certain, but he thought one of them was Chet Small. They made no move to ride closer, and Frank felt no compulsion to ride over to them. He continued on his way, and the last he saw of the pair of horsemen was when he twisted to look and saw them loping southwesterly in the direction of the Small Ranch's home place.

He sighed, straightened in the saddle, and thought back to the bleak, uncompromising expression on Chet Small's face that morning at the jailhouse. If Small or his men could catch the man who had killed their range boss, the odds were greatly against Constable Hadley ever finding the man, or ever hearing of him again. Chet Small was an open-range cowman, as were all the large ranchers in Copperdust Valley, which meant they had been dispensing range-law justice for a great many years and would not hesitate to dispense it again in a case of this kind. While Frank had grown up believing in that kind of raw justice and was not entirely averse to it even now, he had nevertheless taken an oath as a peace officer to uphold the written law.

It seemed complicated, but it wasn't—not to a man of Frank Hadley's philosophy. But he wanted to find the killer, too, mainly in order to determine what exactly had happened back there where Howard Beasely had died.

By the time he reentered town by the back alley and passed the cribbed and patched old public corrals, it was dark. Suppertime was past, someone was playing the piano up at Bud Arlo's place, and the night man had replaced the day man at Tobin's barn, so Constable Hadley got a blank look when he asked about someone hiring a rig the day before.

He went over to the café, got a sour look from the unshaven and overweight café man, ordered a supper of steak with fried spuds and black coffee, then looked up as another late diner came in from the roadway.

It was Hank Bostwick. They exchanged a nod as Hank loosened his coat, stepped over the bench, and sank down at the counter with a rattling sigh. He turned and said, "I'll never know why I stayed in this damned staging business. When my pa died years back, he left me a real nice shoe store back in Missouri."

Frank nodded sympathetically. "What's wrong?"

"Some son of a bitch ran off six or eight head of company horses from our fenced sections in the foothills," grumbled Bostwick, and looked sorely at the café man, who looked balefully back as Bostwick ordered. "Steak and spuds, coffee, and apple pie if you got it. Have you?"

The irritated café man, who loathed late diners, said, "No!"

Hank sat looking up, getting redder by the minute. "Well, why in hell don't you?"

"Because I been too busy, that's why," stated the café man.

Hank drummed on the counter for a long moment staring upwards, then he said, "Crap! Go get my dinner —get out of my sight!"

The café man was quivering with indignation as he turned away, and Frank Hadley said, "I'll go look for your horses in the morning, Hank."

Bostwick answered grumpily, "You won't find 'em, Frank. Small Ranch hasn't found theirs, an' they lost 'em the same night."

For a moment the constable sat in silence gazing at his friend. "Small Ranch had some horses stolen, Hank?"

"Yeah. Last week. Same night, I'd guess, when mine was run off." The stage company superintendent turned. "They didn't tell you?"

"No, and that don't make much sense, because Mr. Small was in town to see me early this morning."

Hank's interest rose. "I wonder why not? From what I heard around town, they lost about thirty head of good using-stock horses."

Frank wagged his head and resumed his meal. It bothered him more than he wanted to say, right at this moment, that Chet Small had not mentioned having his remuda raided, because that could have something to do with Howard Beasely getting killed, even though there may have been a week between one event and the other.

He finished eating, paid up, and went out into the cooling night. He crossed to the jailhouse to sling his gunboot from its wall-peg, make sure the fire was dead in his stove, then to lock up for the night.

It did not require great brilliance to guess why Chet Small had said nothing about having horses stolen from him last week; sure as God made little green apples, the Small

Ranch riding crew had caught themselves a horse thief, or maybe two or three, and had hanged them.

He headed for his quarters at the rooming house, thinking that he might ride over there tomorrow, ask Mr. Small about those stolen horses, and raise mild hell because he was not informed that there had been a horse raid. In fact, it annoyed him too that Hank had just casually mentioned it at supper tonight, when he had also been raided last week. It seemed almost as though people had no confidence in Frank's ability to do his job, to go manhunting for horse thieves. While technically it was true that he had no authority beyond the limits of the town, actually, as the only full-time lawman in all the country bounded by the Copperdust Hills, he did about as much law enforcement on the range as he did in Blythe.

CHAPTER 6

A Nice Morning

THE next morning after breakfast, Frank Hadley walked to the south end of town seeking Jasper's day man. He found him out back at the wash-rack, sluicing off a gray mare that had spent most of the night lying down in her stall and had the inevitable "coffee stains" that didn't always show up on darker hides but showed up glaringly on grays.

The hostler said that the man who had hired the rig the day before had been a rangy, brown-haired man with pale gray eyes who did not smile and who had used the barest minimum of words to make his wants known. The day man added, "I seen him a while back comin' out of the harness shop."

Frank Hadley returned to the roadway and walked northward. The saddle and harness maker was a gnome of a man—bent, old, taciturn by nature—and when he looked up and saw who his visitor was, he turned, aimed at a coffee tin behind the counter, and spat amber before shifting his cud of chewing tobacco so he could say, " 'Morning, Constable. What can I do for you?"

"A man walked out of here a few minutes ago."

The old man nodded and turned to gaze at a saddle propped on its swells in a corner behind his work table. "Left that outfit. It's got mud on it and looks to me like it was left out in the rain. He wants it cleaned up an' oiled."

The aged, shrewd eyes came back around. "Is he a wanted man, Constable?"

Frank shook his head while leaning to study the saddle. "No. What name did he give?"

"Didn't," stated the old man. "I don't need no name when a man pays in advance."

"Did he say where he was staying?"

The taciturn old man shook his head. "Nope. Neither one of us said much. He told me what he wanted, I told him the price, he paid it an' walked out."

Frank eyed the harness maker, thinking that he should have expected something like this. The stranger did not talk much, and neither did the old man. Then the old man abruptly said, "I saw him goin' into the rooming house a while back. Maybe he's still up there."

Frank nodded and walked back out into the warming new day, gazed up and down the roadway, then went hiking on up to the boardinghouse. Whether he found the man he was seeking or not, he would at least learn his name.

The proprietor, who was also Frank Hadley's landlord, was in the big dingy kitchen playing solitaire when Frank walked in. The proprietor was a heavy man who shaved once a week and rarely wore anything on his feet but carpet slippers. He enjoyed his present situation because he was married to a woman fifteen years younger than he was, who was as strong as an ox and worked like a horse while her husband sat in the kitchen reading, eating, or playing solitaire.

The slovenly man smiled broadly. "Frank, you're in luck. I just set a fresh pot of coffee to boil. Pull up a chair."

Hadley pulled the chair around but ignored the pot on the woodstove. "You got a new roomer, Wes. Tall, rangy feller who doesn't talk much and has—"

"Yeah. His name's Mark Forrest. You didn't have to

describe him. He's the only new roomer we've had in two weeks." The landlord's eyes narrowed. "Is he a fugitive, Frank?"

"No. Not as far as I know anyway." As the constable arose to depart, he smiled. "Thanks for the offer of coffee, but I don't have the time right now. Is Mark Forrest in his room, do you know?"

"Got no idea. He might be. I ain't been down the hall yet this morning, been too busy here in the kitchen. You might go see, though; he's in room number eight."

Frank went back down the dingy hall, past his own room, and down to number eight. He knocked three times without getting a response, then tried the knob; the door was locked. If Mark Forrest was in there, he did not want company, but the chances were just as good that he was not there. Frank returned to the roadway.

There was no man answering the description of Mark Forrest in sight. A light ranch wagon was drawing up in front of the mercantile store, and a pair of rangemen were walking their horses into town from the north end, talking as they rode along. Otherwise, except for several women with net bags on their arms heading for the general store, the roadway was quiet. It would probably remain that way until later in the day.

Frank walked south in the direction of his office. He met Hank Bostwick in the corral yard gateway arguing with a Mexican-looking yardman. When Hank saw the constable, he waved the yardman away, shoved big-fisted hands deep into his trouser pockets, and did not smile as he said, "Hey, I thought you were goin' up yonder this morning to look for my stolen horses."

Frank looked straight back, also unsmiling. "Why didn't you tell me last week you'd been raided, when the damned horses were stolen?"

Hank did not yield. "I would have, if I'd known it. Two yardmen went up there yesterday to bring back some animals. That's the first I knew I'd been raided."

Frank was slightly mollified. "All right. Then how did you know your animals were stolen the same time Chet Small lost some stock?"

"Those two fellers I sent up there—one was that cantankerous Messican I was just talkin' with when you came up—those two boys are about as good at readin' sign as anyone I ever knew. They found the break in the fence, picked up the tracks, and followed them right on over where the horse thieves scooped up some of Mr. Small's loose stock, then cut up into the mountains."

As Constable Hadley fell silent, the stage company superintendent stood gazing at him. Eventually he said, "What the hell's bothering you?"

"Did you hear that Howard Beasely was shot and killed up near the foothills?" answered Hadley.

Hank Bostwick's rugged countenance underwent an abrupt change. "Howard? What in hell happened? You don't mean horse thieves got him."

Frank frowned. "A week after they stole the horses?" Then Frank shrugged his powerful shoulders. "I don't know what happened, Hank. But Howard's down in the icehouse and Mr. Small isn't very happy."

Bostwick shifted position slightly and glanced down the road before speaking again. "This damned territory's goin' to hell," he said. "Horse thieves, gunmen; what'll be next? Probably one of my stages'll be robbed." He swung bitter eyes back to the lawman. "What we need is some vigilantes." He made this statement with strong emphasis because he knew what Frank Hadley's reaction would be. And he was correct.

"Vigilantes!" exclaimed the constable. "We won't have any damned vigilantes in my town, Hank!"

* * *

Across the road in front of the saloon where those two range riders who had entered town from the north end were tying up, a slouching man watched everything they did. When they ducked around the rack to enter the saloon, the slouching man straightened up and said, "Gus Carter."

One of the riders paused and turned. He was a coarse-featured individual with small eyes, a thick nose, and a jaw that was too massive and heavy for the rest of his features. He looked at the slouching man blankly. "Yeah. What d'you want?"

"You son of a bitch," said the rangy, faded man with the pale gray eyes, "I want you!"

Neither Carter nor the other rangeman moved. They gazed at the stranger in complete surprise; the stranger was going to fight. Neither of the rangemen had had any inkling. The stranger had caught them totally unprepared.

He did not raise his voice nor more than flick a glance at Gus Carter's companion as he said, "You—beside Carter —you pitch that six-gun into the road and keep out of this. Do it!"

The second man blanched, shot a look at Gus Carter, at the faded, pale-eyed man fifteen feet away, then lifted out his holstered Colt and tossed it backwards. It landed beneath the feet of the horses at the hitch-rack.

Carter was finally recovering. He was a man of no imagination, no genuine intelligence. He was a bully: a blustery, tough-acting man who could be, and often was, physically violent when he thought the danger to himself was minimal. He clamped his heavy jaw closed, stared at the man challenging him, and said, "Who the hell do you think you are? I'll break your gawddamned neck."

The stranger jerked his head very slightly. "Step away from the horses." When Carter did not move, the other man said, "You murdering bastard, *step clear of those horses!*"

Gus Carter remained rooted in place. He had no intention of moving, of doing anything that might interfere with his draw. At that range he could not miss, and he knew it.

His companion, no longer armed, and positive he was looking at the face of death fifteen feet off, shuffled his feet slightly to get a little farther away, over closer to the saloon's rough old log wall. He craned around, saw Constable Hadley across the way and northward, over in the corral yard gateway talking with Hank Bostwick, and thought of risking a hand gesture, then decided against it. A hand movement at this moment could get a man killed.

He looked back to where Carter and the faded man were poised to kill. Carter was concentrating on the man on the boardwalk. He said, "Who the hell are you?"

Instead of answering the question, the faded man said, "You no-good son of a bitch!"

Carter's right arm sank perceptibly, along with his right shoulder. The faded man gave him that much of a lead—one second—then swung his body sideways, drew, and fired. The muzzle blast of one gun, then a second gun, blew the town's morning quiet apart. The two tethered horses pulled back in terror. One broke his reins, spun, and bolted north up the road.

Frank Hadley and Hank Bostwick were stunned. So were several other people who had been strolling the roadway. The disarmed rangeman stopped breathing to stare. Gus Carter was on his back, one hand dangling over the edge of the walk. The stranger was motionless, looking downward, holding a smoking gun at his side. Behind him, along the front wall of the saddle shop, there was a long, deep, raw gouge where Carter's slug had missed the stranger and struck wood beyond.

People emerged gingerly from store doorways to peer around. Frank came swiftly across the roadway, trailed by

Hank. When he got there and saw the man with the smoking gun, he stopped, stared at Carter, then swore to himself. As he reached for the smoking Colt, he said, "Is your name Mark Forrest?"

The faded, gray-eyed man looked up. "Yeah." Then he pointed to the cowboy over along the log wall, who was white to the eyes. "It was a fair draw, Constable. Ask that man."

Frank merely glanced at the white-faced man, then pointed with a stiff hand. "Across the road, Forrest. Hike ahead of me down to the jailhouse, and if you get clever, I'll shoot you with your own gun. Walk!"

CHAPTER 7

The Aftermath

THE town was excited. It was also agitated. There had not been a killing in Blythe in six or seven years; longer than that if one limited the shooting to broad daylight, mid-morning in fact.

A gangling boy caught the loose horse and led him back in front of the saloon by his broken reins. Then the youth stood stonelike, mouth agape, while he watched Hank Bostwick supervise the lifting of the dead rangeman. Hank growled a question at the unarmed cowboy. "Which horse'll carry him?"

The cowboy said, "The tied one. That's his horse, the one he was riding."

Hank and his yardmen spilled Gus Carter belly-down across the saddle and made certain the girth was tight, then tied Carter so he could not slide off. While the tying was in progress, Hank walked over to the cowboy and said, "You work for Mr. Small, don't you? Seems to me I've seen you and that dead feller around town."

The cowboy was young, perhaps twenty or not quite. What he had just witnessed would not leave him for days; he was not in the category of someone like the seasoned Hank Bostwick, who now said, "What caused it?"

The cowboy wagged his head. "I don't know. There was that feller standing at the end of the building. I didn't much notice him until we'd tied up and got down. Then he come ahead a little and called Gus."

"What did he say?"

The cowboy gently wagged his head again, still in a shocked daze. "I don't know; somethin' about Gus being a murderin' bastard. I think it was somethin' like that."

Hank looked steadily at the white-faced horseman. "Well, you might as well take your friend back to the ranch. Gawddamn, that's two in one week for Mr. Small."

People were congregating on both sides of the road, not very many of them but enough to make up three or four small groups. The largest group was in front of the mercantile establishment, and it included the proprietor and his clerk, both wearing flour-sack aprons tied at the middle.

Across the road the jailhouse door was closed. People had seen Constable Hadley herd the killer in over there, and they speculated a lot, but no one made any move to approach the building. Which was just as well, because Frank would have slammed the door in their faces.

He was angry all the way through. Not entirely over the killing, although he was furious about that, but also because if he could have found Mark Forrest first, there would have been no killing. At least, that was what he was thinking while watching the faded, gray-eyed man empty his pockets into his hat over at the desk.

When the pockets were empty, Frank pointed downward. "Lift your pants legs."

Mark Forrest leaned over and obeyed. Frank saw no hideout gun and no boot-knife, so he started toward his desk chair as he said, "All right, let 'em down. Now go sit on the wall bench over yonder." Frank sat down and stared at his prisoner. "How did that happen?" he asked flintily.

Forrest was an impassive man with deep-set eyes, good features, and a hard, bitter cast to his wide mouth. He gazed straight back at Constable Hadley. "The son of a bitch drew," he said quietly, "and I beat him. That's how it happened."

"Did you know him? What started it?"

Forrest leaned back, got comfortable, and did not open his mouth. But neither did he drop his gaze from the lawman's face.

Frank tried a different question. "Where are you from?"

Forrest sat there, looking directly back and not uttering a sound.

Frank considered, then tried again. "Were you waitin' over there for Carter, and if you were, how did you know he'd be along this morning?"

This time, Mark Forrest reached into a shirt pocket, brought forth a new sack of tobacco, and proceeded to open it so he could roll a smoke. He did not open his mouth except to plug in the cigarette and slowly light it.

Frank went after a cup of lukewarm coffee, ignoring his prisoner until he was back comfortably at the desk again; then he studied Forrest. He already knew Mark Forrest did not speak unless he had to. Right now he evidently did not feel that he had to.

Frank leaned on the desk. "Listen to me," he said, with most of the anger out of his voice. "That man you killed rode for a cowman named Chet Small. The biggest, richest range stockman in this territory. That'll be the second man he's lost this week. Forrest, if you got a decent defense, you better tell me because Mr. Small'll have your hide unless what you did this morning was justified."

Mark Forrest trickled smoke, swung calm eyes to the gun rack over along the north wall, and shifted his gaze to a faded lithograph a previous constable had tacked to the south wall. It depicted the heroic and inaccurate *Last Stand of George Armstrong Custer*.

Finally he let his eyes drift back down to Frank Hadley. He did not say a word, and it was clear now that he was not going to say a word.

Frank drank some coffee, then got more comfortable at his desk, eyeing Mark Forrest with a shrewd and speculative gaze. "Day before yesterday you hired a rig, borrowed a shovel, and went up toward the foothills on Mr. Small's range. Mr. Small's range boss, a man named Howard Beasely, got shot and killed up close to the foothills, maybe the night before. Anyway, they found him lyin' up there."

Mark Forrest was listening. His eyes did not leave Frank Hadley's face, and the only thing he did when Frank paused was to inhale and exhale. He did not make a sound.

Frank went on speaking. "Mr. Forrest, I've got the range boss across the road in the icehouse. He was shot at the same close range you shot Gus Carter. I'll tell you something else that just occurred to me—Howard Beasely was not expecting it either. Someone was right there when he rode up. I knew Howard fairly well; I'd say he'd have to be as surprised as Gus Carter was to get shot dead like that."

Mark Forrest moved for the first time. He rose, put both hands behind his back, and strolled over to stand two feet distant, gazing at the *Last Stand* lithograph, smoke drifting lazily upward from his cigarette.

Frank waited for a moment longer, studying his prisoner's tanned, weathered profile with its iron-cast jaw and chin, then rose and reached for his brass key ring. "Let's go." He took Forrest down into the cell room, locked him in, and leaned on the doorway to say, "You're not playin' your hand very well."

Finally Mark Forrest spoke. "Ask that cowboy who drew first. I told you, it was a fair fight."

This time it was Constable Hadley who did not speak. He turned, left the cell, barred the door from the outside, pitched the brass key ring atop his desk, and walked out into the midday sunshine.

Blythe was not yet back to normal, but at least the little gatherings had dispersed as Frank started on a diagonal course for Bud Arlo's saloon. He stood awhile gazing at the place where Gus Carter had died. There was not even dried blood to show for what had happened. The horses were gone from the hitch-rack and, except for an old gaffer soaking up sun-warmth on the bench out front of the harness works, the road was empty. Inside Bud and Hank Bostwick were slightly apart from several other midday beer drinkers, and watched Frank cross toward them with solemn faces.

Hadley asked where the other range rider was, and Hank told him. "We tied Carter over his saddle and sent the other feller back home with him. Why?"

"Because he was a witness," stated Frank, waiting as Bud went to pump up a glass of beer and return with it for the lawman. "Bud, do you know that other cowboy's name?"

"Brady. I think I've heard the other fellers call him Jack." As the barman leaned over, he also said, "You know that other feller, Frank? He was in here a week back; we talked a little about him sittin' at a table over there in the corner without takin' a drink from the bottle. Remember?"

Hadley did indeed remember, but at that time another faded-looking, nondescript rangeman hadn't meant a thing to him. He lifted the glass as Hank asked a question.

"Did Forrest say why he shot Carter?"

Frank drank before nodding. "Yeah. They had an argument. That's all he said. That, and it was a fair fight and that this Jack Brady can prove it was fair. That's all. He sat there like a big stone lookin' at me and not opening his darned mouth."

Hank said drily, "He better open his mouth. I'll bet you a

month's wages Mr. Small will be in town this evening, and I'll bet you another month's wages that when he's through with Mr. Forrest, there won't be enough left of him to shake a stick at."

Frank finished his beer and returned to the roadway to stand thoughtfully under the overhang of the gunsmith's shop. He was willing to believe Mark Forrest had also killed Howard Beasely. Of course, there was no proof of this; there had not been a witness to that first gunshot death. What bothered him as much as the actual killings was why they had happened.

Unless he got the story from Mark Forrest, though, it did not appear that he would get it at all. And that was only one part of Frank Hadley's dilemma; he could not hold Mark Forrest more than twenty-four hours without someone, Small or himself, signing a criminal complaint against Forrest. But a criminal complaint had to be based upon either proof of the commission of a felony or, at the very least, a reasonable supposition that a felony had been committed, with the reasons for that supposition stated. All Frank had was a hunch. Moreover, he knew by now that he was not going to get one word out of Forrest, except the reiteration that he had killed Gus Carter in a fair fight—which Frank believed he had.

He could not hold Mark Forrest beyond tomorrow morning—afternoon at the very latest—and as sure as God made little green apples, when Forrest was released, Mr. Small and his riders were going to be somewhere around, waiting.

Or Carter's bunkhouse mates would be waiting; Carter did not have to have been a popular man on the Small Ranch; all he had to have been was one of them. That was how range riding crews thought, and Frank Hadley knew that as well as he knew his own name.

He went down to the café, got a surly look and gave one

in return, growled for a plate of beans and a jar of coffee to be made up, then ordered his own midday meal and ate without looking up as other men who had no women to cook for them began filing in to take on the load of food that would see them through what was left of the day.

Across the road at the jailhouse, when he took the two plates down into the cell, his prisoner was lying out full length on the bunk, gazing steadily at the thin shaft of sunlight that came through the narrow, barred window in the front wall.

"Eat," Frank said, bending down to shove the little pots under the steel door. As he sat up, Mark Forrest swung his long legs to the floor and returned the lawman's stare, silent and impassive as ever.

Frank said, "If you wanted those two men, Forrest, why didn't you just shoot them out of the saddle? No danger that way."

The lanky man picked up the beans and the coffeepot, took them to the bunk with him, sat down as though Frank did not exist, and settled himself down to eat. Hadley returned to his office, slammed the cell door, barred it, and tossed his hat atop the desk.

Two hours later, when Chet Small and four of his men walked their horses down into town from the north end, people who saw them hurried away to pass the word of their coming. Frank was skiving kindling for his morning fire and looked around only when Small and his riders walked in from out front.

Frank tossed the shaved scantling aside, pocketed his clasp-knife, and went to his desk as he nodded to the visitors, and did not open his mouth.

Chet Small said, "Do you still have him in your cells?"

Frank answered shortly. "Yes."

There had been no preliminaries, and there was no need

for any; Frank knew why Small was here, and Small was not an individual who indulged in very many preliminaries in any case.

"Is there a signed warrant?" Small asked, lusterless little eyes fixed upon Constable Hadley.

"No," replied Frank. "That man behind you, Mr. Small, Jack Brady, he saw it." Frank looked past Small to speak, but the cowman cut in first.

"I'll sign the warrant, Constable. For murder."

Frank stood with words upon his lips for the young cowboy and slowly dropped his eyes to Chet Small. The cowman was standing just across the desk, his gaze fixed on the constable. As Frank exhaled, then sucked back a fresh breath, he said, "You can sign one, Mr. Small. I'll make it out. But you got to offer some kind of proof."

"Jack Brady," stated the cowman in a toneless voice. "He was fifteen feet away."

Frank said, "Mr. Small, Gus Carter got off a shot."

The cowman gave his head a faint up-and-down nod. "Yes. But he was going down when he got it off, Constable. He was jumped by this man Forrest, without any warning and without any reason, and murdered. Jack saw it that way." Small made a little gesture with one hand. "Fill out the paper and I'll sign it, Constable."

Frank did not move. This entire interlude was irritating him. Not simply the way Chet Small had the initiative, nor simply the way Small was issuing orders and compelling events to conform to his desires, but the way Small was putting words into the young cowboy's mouth. Frank's irritation had nothing to do with the man in his cell; as far as Frank Hadley was concerned, Mark Forrest could go to sleep down there in his cell and never awaken again. He regarded the wealthy cowman almost stoically when he said, "I like to talk to witnesses on my own, Mr. Small, not have them brought to me by someone else with their story already fixed." Frank raised his eyes. Young Jack Brady was getting pale in the face. Frank gestured toward his backroom door. "We'll have a little talk," he said, and went over to open the door and wait.

Brady looked desperately around at his employer, then finally over to where Frank was waiting. Chet Small gave an almost contemptuous nod, and Brady went over and entered the storeroom with Frank. As Hadley closed the door, the cowboy said, "That's how it happened, Constable, just like Mr. Small said."

Frank perched upon an old rickety table, shoved back his hat and gazed steadily at the younger man. Finally he said, "Jack, we're talkin' about men getting killed. This isn't like shootin' someone's dog on your range for chasin' calves. I'll tell you something else you might want to think about. If you swear Mr. Forrest into prison, they won't hang him, because Carter got off a shot, too, and someday he'll get out."

"He killed Gus, Constable. We come to town for a beer and the mail, and that son of a bitch was waitin' for us."

"What did he say before he drew?"

"Somethin' about Gus bein' a murderin' bastard. He called him fightin' names. Sure as I'm standin' here, he was waitin' to do just what he done—kill Gus Carter."

"When did Gus draw?"

"Well, I was off a ways—"

"Jack, Gus wasn't goin' down when he fired, the way Mr. Small said. Go look at the gouge his bullet made. It went in a straight line. It wasn't fired from a falling man's gun. You saw Gus draw."

Brady moved in his tracks and shot a look at the closed door. "I saw Forrest draw. He turned sideways at the same time. Gus . . . Gus was more to my left."

"You didn't see him draw because you were watching Forrest."

Brady let his breath out slowly. "Yeah. I was watchin' the other feller."

Frank stood up away from the old table. "Jack, you're not a witness. You just told me you only saw one part of it." He stepped to the door, opened it, and jerked his head for the cowboy to precede him into the front office. Chet Small and the other men were looking steadily at Jack Brady. They ignored Constable Hadley until he went to his desk and said, "Mr. Small, I'll fill out a complaint, but if you sign it, you better have somethin' better than Brady to use, because in the first place he didn't see your rider draw; he only saw Forrest draw."

"That's enough," exclaimed the cowman.

Frank gazed steadily and balefully at the smaller man. "No sir, it isn't, because your man didn't see it *all*; he only saw part of it. But if you want to sign, fine. I'll make out the papers. And if you go to court like that, I'll tell you something else; any lawyer who gets hold of Jack Brady will cut him to pieces."

Chet Small and his men looked stonily at Constable Hadley for a long time, then Small turned abruptly toward the door. As he was preceding his men out, he said, "You make out that complaint, Constable. I'll be back to sign it."

After the door closed, Frank let out a big sigh and went after another cup of coffee, but what he really wanted was a jolt of whiskey.

He was not especially proud of himself, but neither did he feel bad, and if, in antagonizing Chet Small, he had made a worthwhile enemy, at least he had shown Small that Frank Hadley would not knuckle under to him.

The door opened, and Hank Bostwick strode in wearing a scowl. Before Frank could speak, Hank said, "Walk up to the yard with me, Frank. I want to show you something."

Frank did not move. "Show me what?"

"A seal brown horse that's been snake-bit. I'll tell you what I know as we're walking. Come along."

Frank put down the cup he had been holding, swore under his breath, and followed Hank out into the road.

CHAPTER 8

More Questions

THE same two yardmen from Bostwick's corral yard had ridden to the company's pasture that morning and had found the seal brown horse grazing with the company horses. He was weak, but he was able to move a little, on three legs, favoring his badly swollen front leg. The yardmen had brought him back with them. It had taken most of the day because the seal-brown was unable to go far or limp fast.

When Frank finished examining the injury, he shook his head. The horse had shrunk at least two hundred pounds, his hair was rough, and he was feeble, but his eye was good and he held his head up as Frank stroked his neck.

"Rattlesnake, sure as hell," he told Hank, and Bostwick, who had already made that diagnosis, motioned to a stocky Mexican who was crossing the yard. "Joe, make a poultice of salts and hot water; it's a hell of a swelling, but it don't look infected. Don't stall him. He might lie down an' get cast; put him in a corral by himself, with plenty of feed and water."

As the Mexican led the horse away, very slowly, Hank faced the constable. "I'll tell you something, Frank. That's been one hell of a saddle animal. He's got breeding and bottom."

Hadley was wiping his hands on a blue bandana when he answered. "And he don't belong to you."

Hank nodded. "No, but he sure as hell belongs to somebody, and my guess is that whoever owns him will be out there lookin' for him. That wound's been treated; the horse didn't do it by himself."

Frank pocketed the bandana and gazed after the horse, a puckery look beginning to gather the flesh around his eyes. "No saddle, Hank?"

"They didn't bring one in, and they didn't mention one."

Frank turned slowly toward the roadway, visible through the wide, palisaded gateway. "I just damned well might know who owns that horse," he said, and left the yard.

When he got down to the harness shop, the old man who owned the business was drinking sweetened coffee from a beer mug, leaning on his counter and staring blankly at the far wall. He roused himself with an effort when the constable walked in, and put the mug aside, cocking a quizzical eyebrow. He almost never spoke first, and he did not do it now.

Frank leaned on the counter, and the old man guessed his thoughts. When Frank said, "You get that muddy saddle cleaned up?" the old man came right back. "Good as new. That's it yonder on the wall rack."

"It looks fine. You did a good job," stated the lawman; then, after a short pause, he added, "Did you find seal brown hair on the sheep pelts of the skirts?"

The old man slowly wagged his head. "Bay hair," he said, and waited for Frank to speak again. Instead of speaking, Frank stared steadily at the old man, then at the saddle, and back at the old man again.

"No dark brown?"

"None, Constable, just plenty of bay hair."

The old man watched Frank Hadley visibly wilt at his counter; then the constable nodded and left the shop on his way down to the jailhouse.

When he was inside, in the office, he said, "Hell," with

great feeling, and went to shake the coffeepot. Up at the corral yard he had jumped at a guess about that seal brown horse, which Hank Bostwick had failed to do, although Hank had surely remembered Carl Bronson picking up an uncommunicative stranger at the side of the road and bringing him to town.

Frank had been certain the man Bronson had brought to town and the man in his cell were one and the same, and he had also felt almost certain when he had been examining the seal brown gelding that the horse was the answer to the riddle of that range rider being afoot back yonder where the stage driver had found him and where Hank's yardmen had found the horse.

But a seal brown horse did not leave bay hair on the underside of saddle skirts.

He tasted the coffee. It was not only cold; it was acid, too, so he took the pot out back, flung coffee and grounds into the alleyway, refilled the pot, and returned to put it atop the stove—and met Chet Small with one of his tough-looking riders. They had entered the office while Frank had been out back. He put a handful of grounds into the pot, nodded to his visitors, put the pot atop the stove, and turned briskly toward his desk as he said, "I haven't had a chance to fill out the papers yet, Mr. Small, but if you gents'll have a seat, I'll do it right now."

Chet Small made a surprising statement. "Never mind, Constable. I'm not going to make a formal complaint."

Frank stood at his desk eyeing the two men. Small's flaccid, stolid features were unreadable. The rangeman standing to one side of Small was also impassive, but in a different way. His features showed a granite hardness.

Frank sat down, heeded the warning in the back of his mind, and after a moment lifted his eyes to Chet Small again. "Then I can't hold Forrest," he said, watching Small closely. The cowman showed nothing but acceptance. He nodded slightly, as though what Frank had said was what he had expected, and turned toward the door.

Frank stopped the two men. "If a man was thinkin' the quickest and easiest way to handle this matter would be not to sign a complaint so's I would then have to turn Forrest loose because there'd be no grounds to hold him on—then maybe lynch him—it'd be a mistake."

Small and his leathery-skinned, lean range rider gazed stonily at Frank, then left the office and closed the door after themselves.

Frank leaned back, gazing at the closed door. He told himself he might just as well have been addressing a wall, then rose and went down into the cell where Mark Forrest was draining the dregs of his tobacco sack into a troughed wheatstraw paper. Forrest looked up and went on fashioning his cigarette. When he had it lighted, Frank Hadley pitched his own nearly full sack of tobacco through the bars onto the wall bunk as he said, "Mr. Small was just in." He stood waiting, but Forrest trickled smoke while gazing out through the bars and said nothing. Frank sighed. "He changed his mind about signing a complaint against you."

Forrest removed the cigarette and considered its ash, then put it back between his lips. Frank's patience slipped a notch. "I can't hold you much longer. I'd like to. In fact, if I could, I'd sign the papers myself. But not on the kind of evidence Mr. Small has, and that's all there is."

Forrest spoke. "What about that young rider? He was a witness."

"Naw," Frank replied. "When it came right down to the bare bones, he was watching you and didn't see Gus Carter draw. That'd never be good enough in a lawroom."

Forrest's brows climbed. "Why not? That's what they want, isn't it; to make it look like it was murder? He saw me draw—"

"Partner," Frank said patiently, "Gus got off a shot.

There's no doubt about that. Unless that young cowboy actually saw you shoot a man while his gun was still in its holster, it's not murder. The cowboy didn't see Carter draw, so maybe he and you drew at the same time."

"We did," stated Mark Forrest.

Frank's expression turned wry. "Yeah. Since I been in law work, I've heard that a hundred times. In this case, I believe it. But the point is, Jack Brady doesn't qualify as a witness. I told Mr. Small that if they put Brady on the witness stand, any lawyer with sense enough to pour pee out of an open-toed boot could make his testimony look ridiculous."

Frank paused and leaned on the cell bars, gazing in at his prisoner. After a thoughtful moment, he spoke again. "So I got to turn you out."

For a moment the intimation behind those words did not reach Mark Forrest, but eventually it did, and he slowly removed the cigarette, staring straight at Constable Hadley. "And they'll be waitin' out in the roadway—and you'd like that. You likely helped them figure it out."

Frank's temper slipped another notch. He kept silent until the first hot flash had come and gone. "Someday," he said quietly, "someone is going to beat your head soft, mister. Howard Beasely couldn't do it, evidently, but someone can, and they will. Why in hell would I be tellin' you all this if I meant for you to get gunned down out front of the jailhouse?"

Forrest resumed smoking and kept his pale gray gaze fixed on Constable Small, once again becoming as silent as a stone.

Frank straightened up. "I'll explain why I told you. Because I want you to voluntarily stay in this damned cell for another few days."

"What good would that do?" asked the prisoner.

Frank shrugged. "I'm not sure, but, Mr. Forrest, I'm makin' a little headway—an inch at a time, but I'm makin' it—and when I get this damned mess figured out, why, then we'll go on from there. For example, I saw your seal brown horse today. He's here in town, bein' cared for. And the saddle you left at the harness shop—which is why I figure you hired that rig and drove into the foothills a few days back: to fetch back your outfit."

Mark Forrest stood a moment longer, then turned on his heel, dropped the smoke, and stamped on it. Then, his back to Frank Hadley, he returned to the bunk, sank down, and stretched out full length, both arms under his head, staring at the high, narrow little barred window where sunlight shone into his cell.

Frank returned to the office. What he had wanted to determine was whether Mark Forrest did in fact own the seal brown gelding. All he had discovered was that Mark Forrest was the most intransigent son of a bitch he had ever met in his whole damned life.

The day passed without any additional interest for Constable Hadley. He made a final round of the town after full night was down, drank a nightcap with Bud at the saloon, listened to a pair of rangemen from the southeast range trying to harmonize as they plowed their way through the first few lines of "Lorena," and headed for the rooming house.

There the slovenly proprietor was filling lamps from a tin of coal oil and looked up long enough to ask about the man who had hired room number eight. Frank glanced past at the door with an "8" painted on it as he answered.

"He's locked in a cell for that killing this morning in front of Bud's saloon."

The slovenly man put down his coal-oil can. "So that's who the feller was that shot one of Mr. Small's riders. I'll be double-damned. I didn't know that."

Frank was still regarding the closed door. Finally, in a quiet voice, he said, "You got a key to that room?"

The proprietor looked around at the door, looked at Frank, and wiped both hands, then dug in a sagging trouser pocket, and without a word brought forth his passkey and handed it to the constable as he said, "I don't know a damned thing about anyone goin' in there, Frank. Never seen no one an' never heard no one. Leave the key in the lock." Then he went back to filling the lamps.

The door swung inward and, as he had been told to do, Frank left the key in the lock. There was a pair of large saddlebags lying atop the rumpled bed. Frank partially closed the door, approached the bed, and bent over to unbuckle the saddlebags.

Inside, there was one change of clothing, along with the customary shaving and other personal articles. There were also three tins of sardines, a rolled-up ball of fishing twine with two snelled hooks, three red bandanas, a full carton of saddle-gun ammunition, a half carton of six-gun shells, and a honing stone. Below a packet of matches that were wrapped in oilcloth were two letters, one with an indistinguishable name at the top, the other one without an envelope. The second had a hand-drawn map folded into it. The map showed the country between Big Timbers up in Montana and the south desert country of New Mexico; the note with the map said, "I'll be at the springs on the 3rd ready to leave. Your brother John."

Otherwise the saddlebags revealed nothing Frank thought would help him, so he put everything back about as he had found it, locked the door after himself, and went along to his own room, where he slowly shed his boots, hat, and gunbelt while he reflected.

He was willing to believe, now, that there had been two men named Forrest. What helped him reach this conclusion was that note, the saddle, and the seal brown horse. The other Forrest had been riding a bay; that was his saddle at the harness shop. The seal brown horse, which had been struck by a rattler, had been ridden by the man in Frank's cell, the man who had arrived in Blythe on foot.

For a while Frank stood at the only window his room possessed, gazing down the quiet, darkened roadway toward the lower end of town. Mark Forrest could have supplied every answer to the riddle—but he was not going to do it, so if Frank Hadley was going to get answers, he would have to turn them up himself. And he *wanted* answers—not just because two rangemen had been killed, but also because his curiosity had been thoroughly aroused.

He went to bed trying to imagine where the other man named Forrest was, and, shortly before falling asleep, decided to scout the country up where Carl Bronson had found Mark Forrest sitting at the side of the road.

CHAPTER 9

A Discovery

SOMETHING, probably cattle, had knocked down the stake with the red bandana around it where Chet Small's range boss had been found shot to death.

The tire marks of a light buggy were still visible, along with some fading shod-horse imprints, when Frank Hadley got up there and sat awhile considering these things, plus other things such as the lay of the land, the nearness of the low foothill country, and farther back a few miles, the immense, darkly brooding, rugged slopes of forested mountainsides.

To cover the kind of distance Frank had traversed since leaving Blythe, a man had to saddle up in the dark. It had been cold then, and it was still not warm enough to make Frank want to shed his coat, but morning sunlight had other attributes than simply carrying warmth. Frank sat on his patient, big horse, looking along the far-off first ranks of timber. Then he made a more intent examination of the ground. He was not much of a sign reader and never had been. Reading tracks had been just about a lost art when Frank Hadley had been a child. He could make out a little sign, but the grass up in here, while short, was rank; the tracks were old and had been through a rain; and, as Frank finally urged his horse to walk along slowly, he could only occasionally see an impression.

He rode around a long, low land-swell into the foremost

foothills. There were a few larger swells, lifts, and rises on his left and right sides as he walked the horse ahead. There was a large, gnarled oak tree on his right and ahead a hundred or so yards, and between it and Frank there was a knoblike, rounded hill.

He halted, guessed that the tracks he was trying to follow came out of the mountains, and shook his head. He was looking for two sets of tracks. When he was ready to turn back, a pair of big dog-coyotes broke around the low knob of a hill and saw Frank sitting there. They were too surprised to move for a couple of seconds—long enough for him to see dirt on their faces and forefeet—then they turned and ran eastward with their lean bellies inches off the ground.

Frank could not have shot them if he had wanted to; he had no carbine, only his six-gun. He watched them briefly, admired their swiftness, and reined to the right. His horse, in the act of turning, picked up a scent that made him bunch under the saddle and pull back as if to shy.

Frank squared up in the saddle and moved the horse in the opposite direction, which the horse was eagerly agreeable to, since it meant he would be turning away from whatever had upset him. Then Frank rode up past the knob-hill until he was well beyond it and turned right, heading for an old, squatty oak tree where he intended to tie his mount before scouting on foot to see if he could find whatever had spooked his animal.

His horse offered no opposition at all. When they reached the tree, Frank swung off, tied the horse, stepped back to loosen the cincha, and stopped dead still. He was staring at a low oak limb that had the unmistakable gouges left by a rope with a weight at the end of it clearly in sight.

During the autumn, deer hunters made marks like that where they hung a carcass to gut it out. This was late springtime. A chill seeped through the lawman. He turned very slowly, saw a little shallow arroyo on his left not far from the tree, and farther away, over against the east side of the knob-hill, he saw a mound of earth that looked as though it had been settling a little at a time since perhaps even before the recent rainfall.

Frank reached, loosened his latigo, and let the cincha sag, without taking his eyes off the mound of earth. Behind and above him was the rope-scored oak limb. He leaned with both arms over the saddle for a while until some of the cold feeling departed, then he started walking.

He knew what that mound of earth was before he was halfway to it. A grave. There was a wide hole in the near side of the mound where those dog-coyotes had been digging; otherwise, the soft earth had settled completely on all sides of the grave. Frank halted fifteen feet away from the mound. Where those coyotes had been digging, it looked as though the soft earth had been dug in before. He walked a few feet closer, studying the ground until he saw two good boot tracks, both in an area closer to the grave where the grass had been trampled into the ground.

There were other impressions hereabouts, too long for them to have been made by a horse but indistinguishable as boot tracks, because the passage of time and the recent rainfall had blurred them, but Frank was satisfied that men had made them. They were, however, older than the pair of good imprints he stood looking down at.

The grave itself, when he walked up to it, showed marks of recent digging. There was dead grass where earth had been piled as it had been removed. Then the pile had been shoveled back into the grave, leaving a scatter of soft soil over the dead grass where the pile had been. Here he found three more fresh boot tracks. By then he was satisfied that a strong suspicion which had formed in the back of his mind since he had first walked up close was accurate.

A man driving a rented buggy with a shovel sticking up

out of the whip socket had not driven up here just to retrieve a saddle. He had not come up here for that purpose at all. He had come to exhume whoever was in that grave; at least, he had come up here equipped to open the grave and view the remains.

Frank stood awhile beside the grave, then turned to pace back to the oak tree, where he stood a moment or two gazing up where the rope burns showed. Finally he shoved back his hat, turned to set his back to both the tree and grave, and slowly fashioned and lit a cigarette. He let go a slow bluish cloud of fragrant smoke and leaned on his saddle. The drowsing horse cocked an eye around, then faced forward and continued drowsing.

The ramifications of the things he either knew or suspected, which fit together to form an ugly composite, kept him standing there for a long while. He knew who owned this land for miles around. He knew the name of the man in his jailhouse who had killed two men; he knew what had happened out here where the tree and grave were; and he thought he knew why a man had been caught and lynched here.

He did not question the morality of what had happened; he had been coexisting with range law for a number of years. He had matured believing in the necessity for it. But there were some aspects of this affair he did not understand, so after killing the cigarette, he snugged up the saddle, mounted, and aimed southeast again, in the direction of Blythe.

Returning did not seem to use up as much time as heading out had required. Even so, it was late afternoon by the time he handed the reins to Jasper Tobin's day man down at the livery barn and walked over to the café to get a plate of stew and a small pot of coffee. He went to his office, left his hat upon the desk, pitched his coat beside it, and took the food down into the cell room.

Mark Forrest was leaning on the south wall of his cell. He moved only his eyes, watched Frank Hadley stoop to shove the food under the door. Then he straightened up and walked over as if to pick up the meal, halted without stooping, and said, "My twenty-four hours are up, Constable. They've been up since yesterday."

Frank offered no argument. "Yeah, I know. But I'm goin' to hold you a little longer anyway."

Instead of showing anger or protesting, Mark Forrest simply said, "Why?"

Frank continued to stand in the dingy little corridor, gazing in at his prisoner. The man had not eaten all day; when Frank told Forrest what he suspected and what he knew, Forrest was not going to have much of an appetite. Frank started to turn away as he replied to Forrest.

"Eat. I'll be back in an hour or so."

He did not add anything to that, but walked back up to the office, rebarred the cell door, and went to stoke up his stove so the pot of coffee would heat. Then he left a lamp lighted, but turned low since evening was only just now beginning to settle in, and went outside.

Across the road, the clerk at the mercantile company was out front beckoning, so Frank crossed over. The clerk, Wheeler, was a wiry, spare, aging man, small and birdlike. He fished under his apron, brought forth a crumpled bit of paper, and held it out.

"A cowboy was by this afternoon lookin' for you. He told me you wasn't nowhere in town, but he wanted to talk to you—only he didn't want to wait in case you didn't show up today, or maybe until late tonight. He give me that note to give you, then he left town on the south road."

The note had not been placed in an envelope or sealed, and as Frank unfolded it, he could feel the sharp eyes of the clerk on his face. Frank looked down. "You read it?"

The clerk's eyes jumped away and then returned. He

shrugged his narrow, bony shoulders. "Well, he give it to me and all...."

Frank read the note. "Constable, he killed Beasely and Carter. Me and Dusty Billings are next. Luther Grant's already left the country. I'm leaving too. We didn't know the other feller had a partner close by, but what we done was right because horse thieves deserve hanging when they're caught. I know what's going to happen when you let that son of a bitch out of the jailhouse. That's why I'm leaving. Mr. Small says he won't live one day after he's out, but me. I know how he got Howard and Gus and I don't give a damn what Mr. Small says, I'm leaving. If you want to know where his partner is, we buried him near to where we hanged the bastard in the foothills above where Howard got killed. Bill Morton."

Frank refolded the piece of paper, pocketed it, looked up the roadway where a few lights were beginning to appear, then dropped his gaze to the store clerk. "You keep your mouth closed," he said softly, boring a steady gaze into the older man. "Not a damned word, Wheeler, or I'll put you in the same cell with—"

"Constable, for Chrissake, I ain't given to being mouthy. After all these years, you'd ought to know that. I never told a soul today, and I don't expect to tell 'em tomorrow or any other time."

Frank nodded, stepped around the clerk, and went up to Bud Arlo's saloon. The note had named names, but the rest of what it said Frank had fairly well worked out in his mind up in the foothills and on the slow ride back to town.

It was suppertime, which meant the saloon was empty. Business would pick up in another hour or so. As Bud Arlo watched Constable Hadley walk in out of the dusky evening, he reached to pump up two glasses full of beer and set one in front of Frank before nodding and saying, "There's a cowboy around town lookin' for you, Frank. He's been in here a few times; I think they call him Bill something-or-other. Dark-eyed feller, about your height but thinner."

"Bill Morton," stated Constable Hadley, reaching for the beer glass.

"Oh. You saw him?"

Frank drank and then set the glass down. "Well, sort of. Tell me something, Bud, how come this batch of beer is so much better than that batch you were peddling last week and the week before?"

"Frank," Arlo said sharply, "there wasn't a damn thing wrong with that other batch."

"You used bad water," said the lawman, leaning on the countertop.

"I used the same pure spring water I always use. I get it up in the mountains. But I was tempted not to use it when I went up there last week; there was a damn dead horse in a canyon below the spring. He smelled so bad I damn near turned back."

Frank sipped more beer and gazed pensively at his friend for a while, then said, "Bay horse, Bud?"

"Yeah. Big, breedy bay horse."

"Had a bullet hole in him?"

Bud snorted. "I didn't go within a half mile of him. It's been warm lately, Frank. Bullet hole? Have you been up there?"

Frank finished the beer and pushed the glass aside as he replied. "No. I don't have to go up there. Anyway, this is better beer."

Bud Arlo rolled his eyes and heaved a mighty sigh. "Hell, that's the trouble with folks in this country; they just got no taste for good brew. The only thing I done different with that last batch, I used regular sugar instead of corn sugar."

Frank said, "You see, you did spoil it, didn't you?"

"No, gawddammit, I did not spoil it. I just used regular sugar is all. Anyway, that's something else; you can't depend on freighters. They was supposed to fetch five hunnert pounds of corn sugar to the mercantile two weeks ago—what they brought was a quarter ton of regular sugar, and brought it two weeks late. Care for another beer?"

"No thanks, Bud," said Frank Hadley, smiling a little. "But it's good brew." He winked and strolled back out into the lowering darkness, walked across the road to the jailhouse, and went in to turn up his lamp. Then he got his key ring and went down into the cell room.

Mark Forrest had eaten and was smoking, seated on his wall bunk. Wordlessly, the lawman swung open the steel door and jerked his head. Forrest picked up his hat and rose.

They went to the office, and Frank left the cell-room door ajar as he pointed to the wall bench, then went over to see if the coffee was hot. It wasn't, but it was getting there, so he went to the chair behind his desk, sat down, and gazed at his prisoner.

Forrest gazed back as he said, "You think freeing me at night will give me a better chance?"

Frank shook his head. "I'm not freeing you. I just want you to listen to me, so sit back and get comfortable, Mr. Forrest."

The gray-eyed, raw-boned man regarded Frank Hadley unblinkingly. His expression seemed to suggest that he had acquired respect for the constable over the last couple of days, but when he spoke, he appeared to have just one thing on his mind. "I'm going out of here, Constable. You've already held me longer than the law says you can."

"How come you know so much about what the law can and can't do?" Frank asked, sitting relaxed, without taking his gaze off Mark Forrest. "You been in trouble before somewhere?"

Forrest faintly wagged his head. "No. I was a deputy once, a long way from here."

Frank nodded. "Yeah, up in Montana." It was guess on Frank's part, but Forrest's gaze narrowed perceptibly in the lamplight. Frank then said, "You killed two men—Beasely and Carter. You figure to kill three more. Want me to name them for you?"

"No."

"I'll do it anyway, Mr. Forrest: Morton, Billings, and Grant."

Forrest did not move or lower his eyes. Neither did he make a sound.

"Mr. Forrest, want me to tell you how you got the names of the five men who lynched your brother John? You beat the information out of Howard Beasely, then you gave him the same chance you gave Gus Carter, and you killed him." Frank stopped speaking, leaned forward to plant both large elbows atop his desk as he stared in the direction of the wall bench, and said, "And that ends it. Now you know why I'm not goin' to turn you out."

Forrest straightened up from his forward-leaning position, settled his wide shoulders upon the rough log wall at his back, and sat looking across the room at Frank Hadley. This time Frank was silent. He meant to go right on being silent until Forrest talked, if he had to sit there all night and all day tomorrow as well.

But he did not have to. Eventually Mark Forrest said, "Fair fights, Constable, both times."

Frank did not dispute that. He had not, from the first time he had studied Mark Forrest, believed him to be a murderer. But there was one thing he had not been able to figure out. He said, "All right. They were both fair fights. Tell me one thing, Mr. Forrest—how did you know Howard Beasely was one of your brother's lynchers?"

Forrest hung fire before replying. It seemed for a while that he would not answer, as though he would go back into one of his silences again. Then he spoke.

"There were two words scratched into the ground up where they did their lynching. 'Scar Hand.' I figured my brother wrote that before they killed him. I don't know why any of the others with Beasely would write that. So I sat around town for a while until I saw a man with a scarred hand. Beasely, range boss for the Small outfit."

"And you trailed him," murmured Frank.

"No. I didn't have to trail him. I just went up there and waited for him."

"And kicked the other names out of him."

Forrest shrugged, shifted slightly to become more comfortable on the bench, and did not speak again.

Frank sat a moment or two, then rose to head for the wood stove. "Cup of black java?" he asked over his shoulder.

"Fresh pot?"

Frank turned slightly. "Yeah. Reasonably fresh." He filled two cups, carried one to his prisoner, and when Mark Forrest leaned to accept the cup, Frank smiled downward. "If you try it, I'll give you the lickin' of your life."

Forrest did not try it; he might not even have thought of hurling hot coffee in the lawman's face and attacking him.

When the constable was seated again, Mark Forrest went to work creating a smoke. Frank waited until he had the cigarette half-finished, then said, "What did you do with the horses you stole?"

Forrest stopped working his fingers and stared. "We didn't steal any horses. We didn't even know any had been stolen. We saw some tracks of unshod horses in the lower mountains and wondered what the hell loose stock was doing up in there, but we never saw a single damned horse. Accordin' to the tracks, those horses had been through up in there at least two days before we came down from the rims."

Forrest continued to stare at Frank Hadley for a while, resentment and indignation showing in every line of his body. Then he finished making the smoke and lighted it.

Frank barely sipped his coffee; it was as hot as the hubs of hell. He didn't feel much of a need for it anyway. As he put the cup farther away and raised his eyes, Mark Forrest was studying him through a veil of bluish cigarette smoke. Frank said, "I can hold you now, Mr. Forrest."

"Like hell you can."

"Yeah, I can. You got three more men to kill."

"I didn't say that, Constable. You said it."

Frank smiled thinly. "Maybe that's the law, but in the Copperdust Hills country—well, if you've been a cow-country deputy, you know how folks make up some of the law as they go along, and preventing three more men—maybe you, too—from getting killed is all the reason I got to have to hold you."

"While those murdering bastards get out of the country! Constable, I'll find them. I'll hunt them down if it takes me ten years. *Twenty years!*"

"What will you gain, Forrest? You got some idea that ruining your life will make up for the loss of his life?"

Forrest drained his cup and stood up, looking sulphurously down at Frank Hadley. "You should have been a preacher," he said, and waited until Frank also rose. Then they both trudged back down into the cell room.

CHAPTER 10

A Distant Rider

FRANK knew where the cold-water spring was from which Bud Arlo hauled back bottled water for his beer batches. But even if he hadn't known and had simply been passing through the country, he would have been able to find the dead bay horse simply by following his nose—and some high, lazily spiraling buzzards.

Fate was finally beginning to favor Frank a little. If the handsome, big, breedy bay horse had been shot through the body, perhaps through the heart, there would have been no way to determine that at this late date. But the bullet hole was directly between the eyes in the center of the forehead.

Frank looked at the horse's teeth to determine his age, then went on back two miles to a creek and scrubbed, but the smell lingered in his nostrils even after he was back down out of the mountains, resting his horse in the final fringe of huge, old, black-barked fir trees.

West of him a mile or so was the grave and its accompanying oak tree. To the south was the immensity of Copperdust Valley, while southwest of him and not quite visible was the sprawling home ranch of the Small cattle outfit.

Movement snagged his attention off on his left a fair distance. He dismounted, squatted in tree shadows, and watched as a solitary rider loped along below the base of the mountains on an angling course, evidently aiming to avoid most of that broken foothill country. Frank was in no hurry, and it was pleasant up there among the trees. In fact, it was a very pleasant day, providing a person did not go up where Frank had just been.

He tipped down his hat brim to keep the sun's glare from his eyes, and steadily watched the distant rider. As the moving figure got closer, Frank's interest sharpened. For a mile or two, he could not define what it was that intrigued him, but after that distance had been traversed, he knew what it was. The rider was not one of Chet Small's rangemen; it was a woman. She was wearing a light tan blouse, and she wasn't wearing a pair of those horsehide, pale tan shotgun chaps as Frank had originally surmised; she was wearing a split buckskin riding skirt.

He hunkered like an Indian for almost a full hour watching her. By the time she got roughly parallel to him, she was down-country and almost clear of the foothills. She was in fact about a half mile from the grave, which was hidden behind its little knob of a hill, when she broke out into open country and hauled her horse down to a slogging walk.

She probably could have seen Frank if she had halted and made a concerted effort, or if she had suspected he was up there, because, although forest dappling camouflaged him well enough, he and his horse would have been discernible to someone staring directly at either one of them. But the horsewoman no more than casually glanced northward as she let her horse walk along on a slack rein.

Frank thought he remembered having seen her before. Sometime back, when Chet Small had driven into town, there had been a handsome woman in the rig with him.

That was a pure guess. Not only was she too far away for that kind of an identification to be reliable, but when he had seen her in town, she had offered little more than a glimpse of herself before passing from sight into the mercantile building.

As he watched her grow small in the distance, he stood up, flexed knees that had been cramped too long, and turned to swing up across leather as he speculated about the woman. He had had no time to think about her since that first view. Now, he did think about her, but mainly about how she was connected to Chet Small.

Frank was going to have to meet Chet Small shortly now. Anything at all that had to do with the wealthy cowman interested him.

He lost sight of the woman before he cleared the foothills on his way back to town, and by late afternoon when he left the horse at Jasper's barn, he had also, at least temporarily, lost interest in her.

Hank Bostwick was out front of the corral yard with a clipboard in his hands—talking to Carl Bronson, his top driver—when Frank strolled toward the jailhouse. He saw them and continued on past his office, went up to them and smiled as he nodded his greetings.

The perpetually squinted eyes of the stage driver studied Constable Hadley speculatively. "You been busy around town since I was last here," he remarked.

Hank looked faintly pained, as though he knew what his driver was leading up to and would have preferred that he did not mention the killing over in front of the saloon. But Frank was not offended; he was not very sensitive anyway. "One shooting every ten years isn't bad," he told the driver. Then he said, "Carl, remember that feller you picked up at the side of the road couple of weeks back?"

Bronson remembered. "Sure. What about him?"

"Would you know him if you saw him again?"

"I would."

Frank smiled. "Take a walk down to the jailhouse with me. Hank, excuse us for a while."

When they entered Hadley's office and the constable picked up his key ring, the shrewd, narrowed eyes of the stagecoach driver watched. Then Bronson said, "Is this the same man who killed one of Mr. Small's riders? If he is, Frank, an' I identify him. . . ." Bronson shrugged heavy shoulders. "Y'know, Frank, a man settin' up there drivin' a coach presents vengeful fellers with one hell of an easy target."

Frank scoffed. "Not this feller, Carl."

"He killed a man, didn't he?"

Hadley was unbarring the cell-room door when he replied. "He killed *two* men. But he figured he had a good reason. . . . Come along, Carl, he's not a mad-dog killer."

But as they entered the cell-room corridor, Carl fished forth a voluminous red bandana and held it up as though he meant to use it, covering the entire lower two-thirds of his face. He saw Mark Forrest; their eyes met; then Bronson turned on his heel and walked back up to the office, where he stowed the bandana in a hip pocket. "That's him. That's the same feller I brought to town, Frank."

Hadley held the door until Bronson was out on the boardwalk, then said, "Thanks, Carl. I'm right obliged. I'll stand the drinks next time you're in town overnight."

Bronson smiled back thinly and crookedly. "Don't let that feller out until I'm fifty miles south."

Frank closed the door, went back down into the cell room, and traded stares with his prisoner until Forrest said, "Who was he?"

"A man who got a good look at you before Beasely got killed."

"Constable, I'm not denying the range boss and I shot it out."

Frank pulled out his massive pocket watch, flipped open the lid, studied the spidery black hands, then sunk the watch back into a pocket. "Do you know what happened to your brother's bay horse?" he asked.

Forrest scowled faintly. "What's that got to do with the time of day?"

"Nothing. Not a damned thing. I just wondered what time it was, is all. Well—do you know about John's bay horse?"

"No."

"He's dead."

Mark Forrest's gray eyes darkened a few shades. "I thought he would be. They wouldn't dare put him into a riding string. . . . Shot?"

"Yes. How old was he?"

"Six. A year younger than my seal-brown."

Frank already knew the dead bay horse had been six years old. He had made that determination when he had mouthed him up in that canyon. But he had wanted to be sure; it was about the only way left to identify John Forrest's bay horse. In another couple of weeks, that would be about all that would be left of the animal—bones and teeth.

Forrest said, "Open the door, Constable."

Frank considered the ring of keys in his hand as he replied. "Two of them are gone. You killed two. How many were there?"

"You named them off, Constable. You know how many there were."

"Five," Frank said. "No, I knew that five were implicated. I didn't know whether there were more or not."

"Y'know, Constable, you talk an awful lot. Now open that gawddamned door."

"Mr. Forrest, two are dead, two are gone, and I doubt like hell that you'd ever be able to find them again. That leaves one of them still alive."

Forrest gazed steadily out through the bars at Constable Hadley. "I'll get that son of a bitch, and I don't give a damn if the other two went to the moon. I'll keep huntin' until I find them, too. And so help me, I'll get the one that's left!"

Frank gently shook his head. "No, I don't think you will. I'm going after him first."

Mark Forrest loosened his stance slightly, then turned without another word and went to perch on the edge of his bunk. Frank said, "Forrest, you wouldn't stand the chance of a snowball in hell. If you think Mr. Small isn't going to use you, you don't know his kind at all."

Forrest raised a perplexed and irritated gaze to the lawman. "What the hell are you. . . . How can he use me?"

"He simply has to sit and wait—and keep that last of the lynchers at the home place—and have the other rangemen scatter out. You'll be out of here in a few days. He'll sit out there, and when you go after the remaining lyncher, he'll have you in a wagon on the way up to be buried beside your brother. Forrest, you may be damned good with a gun, and you may be a good hand with livestock, but you don't belong in the same class with a man like Mr. Small. Neither do I, for that matter. I'll fetch you some supper directly."

Frank returned to the office, hung the key ring from its wall-peg, eyed his coffeepot, decided he could do better over at the café, and left the office with nightfall closing in over the town.

CHAPTER 11

A Bad Morning

IT was a fairly long ride to Chet Small's ranch headquarters, and for that reason Constable Hadley had intended to get an early start. He would have, except that Hank Bostwick caught him leaving the jailhouse coated and gloved for riding, and handed him a slip of paper.

"The driver who brings in the mail from up north was handed that note sixty miles upcountry," Bostwick explained. "They got thirty-two horses corralled up at Oroville. . . . Well, you can read the note. It's from the sheriff up there. They got thirty-two horses, eleven with the stage company's brand on 'em, the rest with Mr. Small's mark."

As Hank talked, Frank read the message. The authorities up at Oroville had arrested four men driving a band of horses into an Indian reservation up there without the Indian agent's knowledge or permission. They had the drovers in the Oroville jailhouse because the agent had complained about the trespass; afterwards, when the local sheriff and one of his deputies had looked up the brands and discovered who owned those horses, they refiled rustling charges against the four men and were now holding them until someone from the Copperdust Hills country could come up and identify the horses.

As frank finished reading and stuffed the note into a coat pocket, he raised his eyes. Hank said, "I already sent my head yardman. He left about an hour ago. I guess it's up to you to tell Mr. Small so's he can send someone up there, too."

"What the hell did they trespass on the reservation for? That was askin' for trouble," said Frank.

Hank made a guess. "If they were headin' far north before selling those horses, the quickest and fastest way was to go in a straight line, and that meant right across the reservation. It would be a good gamble, Frank. If they'd got across it and well up into Wyoming or maybe even Montana, we'd never have even heard of those horses again."

Hank paused briefly. Up in front of his corral yard, a couple of yardmen were leaving, walking in the direction of the café now that they had taken care of the early morning stage. Hank frowned as he watched the men, then shrugged and said, "Will you see Mr. Small?"

Frank nodded, then thanked Hank. Instead of heading on down toward the livery barn, he went back into the jailhouse and down into the cell room. Mark Forrest cocked an eye, studied the gloves and coat, then said, "Am I goin' to get breakfast, or am I goin' on another fast until you get back from somewhere?"

Frank ignored the question. "When you and your brother came down from the high country, did you see a lot of loose-stock sign?"

Forrest answered thoughtfully and directly. "Not a lot, no. We saw the tracks of what could have been about twenty or twenty-five horses."

"Goin' up through the mountains?"

"Well, when we first cut the sign, they looked to be heading up that way; but we didn't see the horses, so I got no idea where they went. But I'll tell you one thing. Unless they cut eastward to the stage road and crossed by that route, they were heading into real trouble, because up near the rims there's nothing but black ice, slippery talus rock, and snowbanks hip-pocket-high to a tall In'ian."

"One more question," said Frank, gazing steadily at Mark Forrest. "How long would you guess those horses went north before your brother rode down out of there?"

Forrest frowned, thought, then replied. "I'm only guessing. Maybe two, three days. But we didn't pay much attention, and I'm not much at reading sign. Why?"

Frank did not say why he had asked all the questions, but he repaid Forrest's cooperation by saying, "There's a town about sixty miles north of the mountains—north of Blythe—and I just got word the law up there's locked up four men driving horses from this country, bearing local brands."

Mark Forrest walked closer to the front of the cell and steadily eyed Constable Hadley. For a while he was silent. When he finally spoke, it was in a quiet, dead-flat tone of voice. "All right, Constable. Now I'm goin' to tell you something. When I caught Beasely, I told him I wanted the names of the men who had been with him when they lynched my brother. He said he'd see me in hell. I hauled him off his horse and we tussled. And when I asked him again and he refused to answer, I knocked a little more hell out of him. Then I asked him again, and that time he told me they knew one of the men who had stolen their horses had been astride a big, breedy bay horse, and that when John came down out of the hills—"

"They thought he was one of the horse thieves."

Forrest nodded. "Yeah. And they didn't give him a chance to prove who he was; didn't even give him a chance to fetch them back up where I was nursin' my snake-bit horse; they beat hell out of him and then, while he was barely able to stand, they hanged him. Constable, it was the truth. I went back up and opened my brother's grave. He'd been beaten within an inch of his life. But that was after I let Beasely draw against me and killed the son of a bitch."

"He didn't tell you the other names?"

Mark Forrest smiled bleakly. "No. I'll hand him that."

"Then how did you know Gus Carter was one of them?"

"I caught another of Small's riders. I didn't ask his name."

"And you whipped it out of him?"

"Yes. He wasn't up there, but he heard the talk that night at the bunkhouse."

Frank loosened his coat; it was warmer inside the jailhouse than it was out in the early morning on the roadway. "Tell me one thing, Mr. Forrest. Did that cowboy say Mr. Small sent the range boss and those other riders of his up there to try and find trace of the horse thieves?"

"He did. He told me exactly that."

"I'll fetch your breakfast when I get back," said Frank, and left the jailhouse with the first rays of sunshine showing over the eastern rim of the world.

On the ride out to Small's headquarters, he sifted through what he knew, and it left him feeling sick. By the time he reached the yard, the riders had been gone more than an hour and only the cook and the chore boy were over in front of the big log barn. The constable rode up, nodded, swung down, and glanced in the direction of the main house, where a lazy spiral of smoke was rising from the big parlor fireplace.

The cook—a grizzled, lined man who had not been near his razor in about a week—answered Frank's question by pointing. "He's over there, Constable. He don't usually show up out in the yard until well past daylight."

Frank crossed the yard, shedding his gloves as he walked along. When he hiked up the three wide porch steps, he was pocketing the gloves and unbuttoning his coat. It was still cold, but less so than it had been back in town.

Chet Small did not respond to Frank's knuckle-roll over the door, but the handsome woman he had seen the day before did. She smiled as she said, "Good morning," and stepped aside for Frank to enter. She looked to be about thirty, wore no wedding band, was statuesquely put together, and had warm, large dark eyes and a soft, full, generous mouth.

There was something about her that made Frank wonder if he had not seen her before. Then Chet Small walked into the large, handsomely furnished parlor with its polished rosewood and oak, its expensive leather chairs, and Frank had his answer. The woman resembled Small.

The cowman nodded as he met Frank's gaze. "Constable," he said crisply. Then he said, "My sister, Helen Hill—Constable Frank Hadley from Blythe."

Frank nodded and the handsome woman smiled back. Then Frank faced Small again, still not smiling as he said, "I want a direct answer from you, Mr. Small: did you tell Howard and those riders of yours who went up into the foothills lookin' for sign of horse thieves to lynch that man they caught?"

For five seconds neither the woman nor Chet Small made a sound or took their eyes off Frank Hadley. Frank—standing with his hat in both hands, his coat open, the badge on his shirt front partially in view, and the heavy, low bulge of his holstered six-gun ominously showing—waited.

It was a long wait. Finally, Chet Small turned toward his sister. "Would you leave us alone, Helen?" he said quietly.

She lingered for a moment, then walked away. After another moment Chet Small motioned toward one of the big leather chairs. "Sit, Constable."

Frank did not move.

Small stepped to the raised fieldstone hearth with his back to the dying fire and returned Frank's gaze. "To give a direct answer, Constable—no, I did not tell them to hang anyone. I told them to pick up the tracks and stay on them until they found our horses, even if it took them over into the next valley. I told them if they caught the thieves to turn them over to the nearest lawman—unless there was a fight. In that case I told them to kill every one of the sons of bitches."

When Small stopped speaking, the silence closed down again. The warm, richly furnished room held only one very slight sound: the crackling of the dying fire in the fireplace behind Chet Small.

Frank said, "You knew they lynched a man, though."

Small nodded. "Yes. Howard showed me the horse and the grave."

"And you did not tell me, Mr. Small."

"Constable, you know as much about our kind of range law as I do. When you catch a thief, you serve him with justice."

Frank tossed his hat upon a chair, fished in his pocket for a slip of paper, then walked over with his hand extended as he said, "Read that. It's from the authorities up at Oroville."

Frank watched Chet Small's face as the cowman read the note Bostwick had delivered to Frank. He saw Chet Small reread the note, the second time with a slight expression of puzzlement. Then Frank took back the note and said, "Did your men know how many of those horse thieves there were, Mr. Small?"

"Well, yes. They read the tracks and said there were four of them."

"This here note says they got all four thieves in the jailhouse up at Oroville," stated Frank, carefully folding the scrap of paper and pocketing it without looking up. Then he raised his eyes. "Would you like to know why Howard was killed? And Gus Carter?"

Chet Small stood motionless, gazing at the Constable.

"Mr. Small, the man who killed Howard, then waylaid Gus Carter in town and also killed him, is the brother of the man your riders beat, then lynched and buried up in your foothills, then took his horse back up into the mountains, shot him, and rolled him down a canyon. And, Mr. Small, that man they lynched was *not* one of your damned horse thieves."

Again the heavy silence settled throughout the ranchhouse parlor. Frank went back to retrieve his hat and to stand again in front of the doorway, where he had been standing since entering the house. He returned Chet Small's stare without blinking.

"Mr. Small," he said finally, "if I'd have turned that feller loose in town, you'd have had him killed, too. I got a note from a man of yours who quit and headed out of the country, a man named Bill Morton. I also know the names of every man-jack who was up there with Howard when they killed that feller—and I know Dusty Billings is still around . . . . If you think you're going to get that lynched feller's brother killed for shooting Howard and Gus Carter, you're dead wrong, and I'll tell you why—"

Small broke in. "Just a minute, Constable! I did not order *anyone* lynched. I said, *if* they found the thieves and *if* the thieves put up a fight, kill them."

Frank sighed. "What about a man who was riding down out of the hills, who had never been in this country before, had every right under the sun to be where he was, and had not even seen those damned horses you and Hank Bostwick lost?"

"Constable, until right now I did not know he was not one of the horse thieves—and that's why I wanted the man who shot Howard and Gus. I figured he had to be one of the horse thieves to go after my men for that first killing."

"It wasn't just a killing, Mr. Small; it was a lynching! And regardless of what you thought, your riders hanged a man who didn't even know you had a ranch out here and who never even saw your rustled horses."

Again the heavy silence settled, but this time Frank did not allow it to settle for long. He said, "Where is Dusty Billings?"

Small's lusterless, oily colored eyes grew still as wet stones. "Why do you want to know?"

"Because I'm goin' to haul him back to town with me and lock him up. And the reason I'm going to do that is because I can't hold Mark Forrest another day, or I'll be more in violation of the law than I care to be. I'm goin' to lock Billings up, free Forrest, and keep Billings in my cells until I'm satisfied Mark Forrest is plumb out of the country. Now, where can I find him?"

For the first time since Frank Hadley had begun to speak bluntly, the wealthy cowman shifted his stance in front of the fireplace. He looked to his left, where there were several open doorways, then went to a beautifully carved mahogany sideboard, filled two small glasses with red wine, and wordlessly went over to hand one to the lawman. Frank accepted the glass, then leaned over and put it untouched on a small marble-topped table and watched Chet Small walk back to the hearth, head down. When Small faced around and lifted the glass, Frank said, "It's a long ride, Mr. Small, an' I'd like to get back before suppertime. Where is Billings?"

Instead of answering, Small asked a question of his own. "Can you prove that man Howard hanged was not one of those horse thieves, Constable?"

Frank's temper slipped a notch. "Mr. Small, *I'm* satisfied he wasn't one of them. I'm plumb satisfied he did not even know your name or what any of your livestock looked like, and he sure as hell did not steal any horses off you or Hank.

As for proof—when there's a hearing, and maybe later on a trial—I'll hand over all the proof I can dig up. Now, where the hell is Dusty Billings?"

Chet Small emptied the little glass, turned, and placed it atop the fireplace mantle. Then he went to take down a hat and riding jacket. He put them on while looking steadily at Frank Hadley as he said, "In the bunkhouse. Come along." After they were out on the wide, long veranda with the door closed at their backs, Small said, "Mr. Hadley, so help me God, I didn't even suspect it was not a horse thief they hanged."

Frank was resetting his hat when he answered. "That won't bring him back."

They walked down off the porch with Frank eyeing the massive log bunkhouse, which had a thin stream of smoke rising overhead. Halfway across he said, "Why didn't you send Billings out with the other men this morning, Mr. Small?"

The cowman paused briefly before answering. "I wanted him on the place.... There are chores to be done."

Frank halted. So far he had not believed that Chet Small had lied to him. Now it was different. Large cow outfits had chore boys to do things around the home place; they did not keep back a qualified range rider for that purpose.

Small looked at Frank. "Well . . . ?"

Frank gestured, his face showing more disgust now than anger. "Keep walking."

When they stepped up onto the small bunkhouse porch and their footsteps made a solid sound over the planking, someone inside made a furtive, sliding sound. In the back of Constable Hadley's mind, a shrill warning sounded.

He swept back his coat, jammed it under the shellbelt to leave his six-gun exposed, and instead of opening the door or even rapping on it, he called out.

"Billings, this is Constable Hadley from town. Come on out, I want to talk to you."

For moments there was not a sound from inside, then Frank detected the stealthy opening of a door. Without waiting, he moved past Chet Small around to the back of the structure where there was another small covered porch, which protected the bunkhouse wash rack.

As Frank came around the corner of the building, a man's thick, burly figure appeared, gun in hand. The man was looking in the direction of the rear of the big log barn, and Frank could see why—there was a saddled, bridled horse over there patiently standing where the reins had been looped through a stud-ring. There were saddlebags and a tight bedroll secured to the saddle. In another few minutes, there would have been no one in the bunkhouse or, for that matter, in the ranch yard.

Frank was reaching for his holster when the burly man swung his head and saw the lawman. Without any hesitation, the man fired from the hip. A shower of punky wood struck about where Frank had been. Then the man who had fired broke clear in a desperate run for the tied horse, and Frank stepped into plain view, raised and cocked his Colt, and yelled again. "Billings! Hold it!"

Behind Frank, Chet Small also called to the running cowboy. "Dusty! It'll be all right!"

Frank saw the burly man begin to twist as he shortened his steps, saw the man's gun swinging to bear. Frank fired. The running man fired again and swung to cover the last fifty or so feet to the horse. Frank hauled back the hammer, steadied his weapon against the bunkhouse wall, and yelled out. "Billings!"

This time when the range rider spun to fire, Frank got off the first shot. Billings was punched backwards as though struck by an invisible fist. He fell and rolled, lost his six-gun and his hat, and stopped rolling.

Frank waited without taking his eyes off the downed range rider. Billings did not move; his entire body began to loosen and sag. Frank exhaled slowly, then turned his head.

Chet Small was lying fifteen feet away on his back, with a bluish little hole squarely in the center of his forehead.

CHAPTER 12

The Prisoner

THE shot Billings got off that had missed Frank had struck and killed Chet Small. By the time Frank rode into the livery barn in Blythe that night with the body of Dusty Billings lashed across the saddle seat of the horse that had been tied behind the log barn, he felt worse than he could ever recall feeling before.

He had left the beautiful woman sitting in the parlor of the ranch house gazing at nothing, unable to hear any of the things Constable Hadley had told her. He had sent the old cook and the chore boy to the house to sit with her, then had struck out for town with the dead lyncher. After putting the corpse across the road in the icehouse, he went over to his office, dug out a bottle from the lowest desk drawer, and had two swallows from it. He was putting it away again when Hank Bostwick walked in.

"Saw the light," Hank said, then stopped stone-still at the look on his friend's face. "Frank, you feel all right?"

The constable sat down and motioned for his friend to do the same. The whiskey began working immediately. Frank had not had a meal all day. He tossed his hat aside, pulled out his six-gun, and methodically began plugging out empty casings and plugging in fresh loads from his belt as he said, "Mr. Small is dead."

Bostwick's suddenly indrawn breath made a sweeping sound. "How?"

"By accident. He was standin' behind me when a feller who worked for him decided to fight instead of comin' back to town with me. The cowboy shot at me and hit Mr. Small between the eyes."

Frank finished with the weapon and sank it back into its hip-holster as he leaned with both heavy arms atop the desk gazing across the room. "His sister's out there, Hank."

"His. . . . Oh, is *that* who she is. I saw her in town a couple of times with him and sort of wondered. Who was the feller you was after, Frank?"

"Cowboy named Dusty Billings."

Bostwick shook his head. "Guess I didn't know him. Where is he?"

"In the icehouse."

"Oh. Frank, what in the hell was all this stuff about? First Howard, then Carter, then Mr. Small, and then this cowboy."

Frank's body was loosening all over. He did not feel any better, but he certainly felt more relaxed than he had been at any other time during the day. "I'll tell you sometime, Hank. Did you want anything in particular?"

Bostwick heaved up to his feet. "Naw. Just saw the light on an' thought I'd come pester you for a spell." He got to the door and had the latch in his big fist before he turned, wearing a faint frown, and said, "You look like you need a drink. You don't look too good. See you in the morning."

Frank did in fact consider another couple of swallows from the bottle in the bottom drawer; instead he took down his key ring and went down into the dark cell room, dragging several large keys across the front-wall steel bars. When he reached Forrest's cell, the prisoner was sitting on the edge of his bunk rubbing his eyes. He said, "What's the sense of waking a man from a sound sleep just to eat?"

Frank did not answer. He just unlocked the door, and,

when Forrest looked up, Frank jerked his head and said, "Out."

Back up in the office, Frank did not bother closing the cell-room door, and instead of replacing the key ring on its peg he pitched it atop the desk, then sat down and leaned to dig out the bottom-drawer bottle. "Sit down, Forrest." As he straightened up and put the bottle in plain sight, he went on, "You can wait until morning, or you can leave right now. Care for a jolt?"

Mark Forrest sat on the wall bench looking directly at Frank. "What happened, Constable?"

"That man you wanted, Dusty Billings, the last of the bunch that buried your brother. . . ." Frank took one more small swallow from the bottle.

"What about him, Constable?"

Frank leaned to place the bottle on the far side of his desk, handy to the man with pale gray eyes. Forrest ignored the bottle and kept his stare fixed on the lawman. "He's dead, Mr. Forrest. I went out to bring him in and lock him up, and he made a fight out of it." Frank leaned back in his chair. "That ends it. And Mr. Small, he's dead, too. Got hit between the eyes by a wild shot." Frank stifled a yawn with a great effort.

Mark Forrest said, "That don't end it, Mr. Hadley."

Frank composed his features and sat gazing at the rangy, rawhide-tough rangeman. He understood exactly what Forrest meant by that bitter statement. He sat studying the other man for a moment, then gave his frank opinion. "You are a gawddamned fool. How old are you? About ten years younger than I am—thirty, maybe? You got maybe another ten, twelve good earning years in you, Mr. Forrest. You'll never find the last two."

"Yes, I will."

"No, you won't. They're out of the country by now.

Wherever they start up again, they'll have different names. They'll be riding different horses and, for all we know, they might even head back east. How are you going to find them?"

"By hunting, by lookin' in every bunkhouse and cow camp between here and—"

"That's exactly my point, Mr. Forrest. You won't find them, but when you're my age and all the best years of your life are behind you, you'll still be looking. Only by then you'll be bitter-mean, friendless, ridin' the same damned saddle, and wearin' the same spurs, and someday when you think you've found one of those bastards, someone will kill you." Frank paused, then went on. "For what, Mr. Forrest? Your brother's dead. You settled up for him a lot better'n most people are ever able to—and the law can't touch you because of the way you did it."

"Like I said, Constable, you sure should have been a fire-and-brimstone preacher."

Frank felt that second pair of jolts overtaking the first pair and languished for a moment, relaxed and almost detached in the way he was considering the man opposite him. "Forrest, it was a damned disgrace and an outrage. It was a stinkin', lousy murder any way a man looks at it. But it was still a mistake. Those bastards had no more right to hang your brother than you had, or I or anyone else had. If they'd had a single grain of sense, they'd have been sure first. Hell, you and I would have made sure first. Forrest, it was still a mistake. And you know the rest of it?"

"No. As long as you're talkin' up a sermon, say the rest of it."

Frank's tired eyes kindled a little. "I will. Damned right I will. One gawddamned disgraceful mistake—and five men are dead. For nothing; over a damned mistake. And someday someone'll catch you with your nose where it hadn't ought to be, and that'll make six. Now that sure makes a lot of sense, don't it, you idiot?"

Mark Forrest arose alowly and stood with all his weight on one leg gazing across the desk. "Constable," he said softly, "you're drunk." Then he turned, went back down into the cell room, and clanged the steel door closed after himself.

For a fair length of time, Frank remained slouched in the old desk chair. Then he groped for his hat, dumped it on the back of his head, and rose to blow down the lamp chimney and plunge the entire jailhouse into darkness before making his way out front. This night he did not bother locking the front door.

Around him Blythe was quiet and mostly dark. The lamps were out, even up at Arlo's saloon. Frank wondered about the time. He could have satisfied his curiosity by simply pulling out his pocket watch; instead he turned northward, straightened his shoulders, and began walking up in the direction of the rooming house, holding himself properly erect and moving with slow dignity, his footfalls sending out the only sounds around as they came down hard upon the duckboards.

He made it. The real sensation of being drunk did not fully hit him until he was fumbling with the key to his room, and by the time he got inside, the only thing he wished for in this life was to find his bed.

Under different circumstances his stomach would have sent out acidic reminders that he had not eaten all day—but not tonight. When he awaked the following morning with the sun already well above the horizon, his stomach made its location known, but not by desiring food—rather, by desiring great amounts of cold water.

He felt tired, but by the time he had shaved and dressed, the tiredness had either departed or turned into something else. As he stepped forth into the sun-bright roadway and saw the steamy front window of the café a couple hundred yards southward, he was ready to eat, and to fetch food over to the jailhouse—in case his prisoner was still there, which he doubted.

The liveryman, Jasper Tobin, was sucking his teeth out front of the café when Frank got down there. Jasper turned a bland gaze on the constable. "I heard you brought a feller in last night and stored him in the icehouse."

Frank stopped and looked at the raffish, unshaven, paunchy liveryman. "Jasper," he said gently, "if folks got paid in this life for bein' nosy bastards, you'd be able to buy us all out."

The words were offensive, but the steady, dispassionate gaze accompanying them was less offensive than it was cold with displeasure.

Jasper straightened up, smiled weakly, and said, "Friends can talk to friends a little, can't they?" Then he stirred up dust in the roadway, hastening to the opposite side on his way back down to the livery barn.

There were seven or eight men eating at the counter, but except for an occasional snort made by a coffee drinker or a fork or knife striking pottery, the room was as silent as the inside of a well.

Mark Forrest was hunched over a big platter of meat and fried potatoes, ignoring everyone else, and the other diners were going to great lengths to pretend he was not there among them. They knew him; everyone in town knew Mark Forrest by now, even the café man who had probably never served him before.

What they knew most graphically was that he had waited until Gus Carter had appeared, then had deliberately and cold-bloodedly challenged Carter and shot him to death. Fair fight or not, people did not cherish the company of a man who would do something like that. They feared him.

Frank sank down beside Mark Forrest. They exchanged a nod, and when the café man came, his surliness less marked this morning—perhaps because, like his patrons, he was conducting himself with great prudence—Frank jerked a thumb. "Whatever Mr. Forrest was having." He looked around, got a few circumspect nods, returned them, and swung in the opposite direction as Mark Forrest said dryly, "You ever lose a prisoner in your jailhouse from starvation?"

Frank leaned on the countertop. "Not very often. How's your horse?"

"I don't know. Where is he?"

"I told you. He's up at the stage company's corral yard. They'll take as good care of him as anyone can."

"How do I pay them?" asked the unshorn, gray-eyed rangeman.

Frank reared back so the café man could slide his breakfast platter into place. "I don't remember anyone mentionin' pay," he replied to Forrest, and reached for his eating utensils. "I hope to hell you don't expect to stay around Blythe until that horse is ready to travel."

Forrest ignored that. "I looked at the two fellers in the icehouse. When are they goin' to bury them?"

Frank had no idea. "That would normally be up to Mr. Small, but since he's dead. . . ." Frank ate, decided the meal was better than he usually got at the café, and relaxed slightly.

"It's a nice place," Forrest said quietly, almost casually.

Frank looked up. "Blythe? Yes, I've sure been in worse places." He continued to chew and gaze at the man beside him. "What's on your mind, Mr. Forrest?"

The lanky man rose, dumped silver coins beside his empty plate, and turned to depart as he said, "Nothing."

Frank ate, topped off his meal with two cups of coffee, paid up, and went outside. Across the road his jailhouse door was ajar. He went over there and found Mark Forrest smoking a cigarette while sitting in a tipped-back chair. When their eyes met, the rangeman said, "My gun and other stuff, Constable."

Frank brought forth Forrest's hat with its contents, handed them over, then went to his desk drawer for the shellbelt, which was coiled around the worn old six-gun in its shiny brown leather holster. As he handed these things to the cowboy, their eyes met and Frank said, "How drunk was I last night?"

For the first time in many days, Mark Forrest's expression lost most of its granite hardness. "Constable, when I left you, you couldn't find your rear end with both hands."

Forrest stood up to deftly swing the shellbelt around his lean middle, catch the big buckle and make the belt fast. Then he lifted and settled the heavy holster with its weapon. Afterwards he eyed Frank Hadley for a moment in silence, nodded, still without speaking, and walked out of the office. He needed a bath, a haircut, and a change of clothing.

Frank went to the desk, sat down, and fished for his makings. As he worked up the cigarette, a series of unpleasant recollections returned. He lit up, leaned forward staring at the opposite wall, then shook himself like a dog coming out of a creek and rose to make a round of the town.

CHAPTER 13

A Matter of Conscience

THAT youthful range rider who had been with Gus Carter the day Carter had been killed rode into town about noon, got the ranch mail, and picked up several saddlebag-sized items at the mercantile company. After buckling down the flaps behind his cantle, he leaned on his horse's rump and eyed the jailhouse.

He seemed to be of two minds about going over there, and apparently he decided not to, because he unlooped his reins and had started to turn the horse when Frank Hadley came along.

They exchanged an unsmiling look. Frank nodded, and the young cowboy turned back to the hitch-rack as he said, "They're sendin' in a wagon for Howard and Dusty and Gus."

Frank accepted that without comment.

"They're goin' to bury them and Mr. Small at the ranch cemetery this afternoon."

Frank leaned on an overhang-upright. "How is Mrs. Hill?"

"Well, I only seen her once since we come back from the range last evening, but I guess she's all right."

Frank studied the youth. He remembered his name, Jack Brady, and also remembered how he had fought a battle with his conscience over being Chet Small's biased witness to the Carter killing.

"Jack," the constable said quietly, "tell me something. You were at the ranch and would know the answer. Beasely knew it, and so did Mr. Small, but they took it with them."

"Well, Constable . . . if I can."

"Those horses were rustled three or four days before the riding crew lynched that feller named John Forrest. Most folks would have figured after that long a time the thieves would be out of the country—but Howard and the others grabbed John Forrest and lynched him anyway. How could that happen, Jack?"

The youthful cowboy's gaze drifted up to the corral-yard gate and to the opposite side of the road; for a while he said nothing. Then he looked back at Frank Hadley and said, "Mr. Small put up a bounty."

"You mean for the horse thieves?"

"Yeah. I was over at the shoeing shed when he come down there from the house. Howard, Gus, three or four other fellers was also there. Mr. Small was like an iceberg when he was mad, and that day he was mad. He said he'd give two hunnert and fifty dollars for any of the bastards who stole those horses, dead or alive, and we didn't have to be picky about which way we got 'em."

Frank shifted position slightly. "Jack, that feller wasn't one of those horse thieves."

"I know. I didn't know it at the time, though. I wasn't up in the foothills that day. Howard had sent me east with the wagon to grub out a couple of sump springs that was silted in. That night after supper when some of us was loafin' down by the barn, Gus told me they'd caught one and hung him. He said Mr. Small was goin' to ride up where they'd buried the feller in the morning, then he'd pay the bounty and they could split it among theirselves."

Frank looked steadily at the younger man. "Howard was along?"

Jack Brady looked straight back. "Yes. But Gus an' me, we rode together a lot. I guess I was about the only feller on the place who got along with him very well—an' there was times when I didn't like him a lot—but we got paired off a lot, so we was friends. He told me he figured Howard wouldn't want to hang the feller, so he told Howard he recognized the man and the big bay horse. Gus was in the foothills the night the horses was stolen. Howard had sent him up there after dark to look for a damned bear that'd been comin' down out of the mountains every night for a week or so, killin' baby calves. Gus told me he swore up and down that stranger on the big bay horse was the same man he seen runnin' off the horse with some other fellers that night."

Frank sighed. "Did Mr. Small pay the bounty?"

"Yeah. Gus showed me his share. In fact, the day that feller killed him out front of the saloon, we'd rode into town to get the mail and spend a little of Gus's bounty money at the saloon."

Frank straightened up off the upright post. They were all either dead or gone, so there was no way to verify this story.

There was no reason that Frank could imagine for Jack Brady to make it up. In fact, what inclined Frank to believe it was his recollection of how young Brady had struggled with his conscience before and had finally ended up telling the truth about the Carter killing.

Brady interrupted Hadley's thought. "Constable, we lost a lot of riders lately. You can't run an outfit the size of the Small Ranch with less than half a riding crew, an' you can't make one work without no range boss an' no owner. Yeah, I know, the lady's Mr. Small's heir and all, but you've rode; you know most men won't ride for a cow outfit run by a woman, even if she knows, and this lady sure as hell don't. She's a widow woman; she came from back east somewhere after her husband died. She can ride pretty fair, but any darned fool can do that. Runnin' our outfit takes more savvy than she'd have in ten years."

Frank's thoughts slowly came around to what the young rangeman was saying, and his first reaction was to disclaim any concern, but when he thought back to how he had left Helen Hill last night — numb with shock, too stunned to speak or even to recognize him when he stood before her — it troubled him to think of how helpless she truly was.

He cleared his throat, glanced up the road, and saw Mark Forrest emerge from the tonsorial parlor freshly shaved, shorn, and quite presentable, then looked at Jack Brady again. "Who's left out there to fill Howard Beasely's boots?" he asked, and got a slow negative head-wag for an answer.

"Three fellers and me, the cocinero and the chore boy — and her. That's everyone. An' two of those other riders were talkin' about quittin' last night in the bunkhouse. Me, I been sort of thinkin' the same thing since yesterday. Only I hate to go off an' leave that lady when she needs rangemen as much as she sure as hell does right now. None of us got range boss savvy."

Frank had no answer. His responsibility had begun and ended with solving the mystery of that lynched stranger and identifying those who had hanged him. It might have gone further, except that the participants in that murder in the foothills, the ringleaders at any rate, were now all dead.

He said, "I'll keep my eyes open, Jack. There's bound to be someone around who can hire out to her as range boss."

"We'll need at least three more riders, too."

Frank nodded and turned to enter the general store for a fresh sack of tobacco. When he glanced around a little later, the place at the hitch-rack where Brady and his horse had been was vacant.

He returned to the jailhouse, fired up the wood stove, and set the coffeepot atop it. He turned toward the barred front window at the sound of a medium-weight rig coming up through town from the south and watched Carl Bronson tool his stagecoach directly up the center of the wide roadway, horses at a slogging walk, chain-harness rattling, the swaying, faded red body of the stage itself layered with road dust.

He remained by the window after Carl had gone past. Mr. Small had not said a word about offering a bounty. Possibly, by the time he had had to pay it, he had realized that he might have contributed to a murder. Maybe not; maybe he had believed his men had indeed caught and hanged a horse thief—but who in his right mind, providing he had spent his life around livestock and all the pleasant and unpleasant events that occurred because of livestock, would truly think a horse thief would return to the country where he had stolen a big band of horses, riding the same mount, coming down the same trail? And who would believe that a perfect stranger in the area, three days later, could not have been exactly that—a complete stranger to the territory?

He turned slowly toward the desk. Well, hell, he told himself, he was never going to know all the answers. No one ever knew them all, but lawmen in particular never did. He sat down. As for Helen Hill, it was not his job to become involved with things like that. Still, he had to return to the ranch for the dead men's personal effects in order to see if he could locate next of kin who had to be notified of the deaths; it could not hurt simply to look in on her.

Carl Bronson appeared in the doorway, wind-burned, bundled in a worn sheep-pelt coat, still wearing thick muleskin driving gloves, and still looking dusty. He smiled and glanced in the direction of the open cell-room door. "You let that feller out?" he asked, moving toward a chair along the front wall beside the door.

Frank nodded. "Yeah. I was only holdin' him until I

could corral the feller he was after. And that feller's dead, so I turned Mr. Forrest loose."

"Is he still in town?"

Frank's eyes puckered slightly with tough amusement. "I told you, Carl, he's not a mad-dog killer. Anyway, the way you hid behind that bandana, he wouldn't recognize you."

Bronson slowly unbuttoned his thick coat, then tugged off the gloves and got more comfortable in the old chair. "I can tell you a little about that feller, Frank. Day before yesterday when I was up near Oroville, I met a feller at the trading post having a drink who knew the Forrest brothers in Montana. I never paid much attention until I got back down here and Hank told me what this feller's name was. They were top hands; they've done it all, from freighting to staging to straw-bossing. This man rode with them at two different cow outfits. He said they were damned decent men, both of them."

Frank did not doubt any of what the whip had said. Clearly, Carl Bronson did not know there was now only one of the brothers alive. Frank went to the stove, drew off two cups of black coffee, handed one to Bronson, and went back to his chair.

He'd had a sudden thought while listening to Carl Bronson, but after returning from the stove, his better judgment told him it would not work. Mark Forrest would never go to work for the outfit he held responsible for his brother's death, no matter whether the actual killers were still there or not.

Bronson sipped coffee, then said, "Did you ever figure out why this Forrest feller killed that man who rode for Chet Small?"

Frank half-drained his cup. He was tiring of this; nor was it the first time someone had asked questions he did not care to answer lately. "I guess it'll all come out someday," he said, and smiled as he drained the cup and reached for the hat atop his desk and stood up.

Carl gulped the last of his coffee and also rose. "If you're around tonight, you can buy me that drink for identifyin' that feller, Frank. I'll be lyin' over for two days in Blythe." Then Bronson smiled and departed, leaving Frank to sink both cups in a bucket of water he kept for that purpose behind the stove.

When he went out into the road and studied the position of the sun, it seemed probable that he could make the ride out to the Small place and, with any luck at all, get back to town this evening before the café man closed up for the night.

An earlier start would have helped, but earlier he had not made up his mind to go out there. Not this soon, anyway.

CHAPTER 14

Four Dead Men and a Woman

HE did not see the wagon they had sent from the ranch for the bodies from the icehouse, but when he was about two-thirds of the way out, he saw a top-buggy coming on a southwesterly course. It was too far ahead for an identification to be made, but for lack of anything else to watch as he rode along, Frank idly speculated about the outfit and whoever might be driving it.

When he got to the yard, there were two rangemen in the barn as he stepped down to tie up, and one of them came to the wide opening to nod somberly and say, "Good morning, Constable."

Frank returned the greeting, shucked his gloves, and headed for the bunkhouse. Jack Brady and the tousle-headed young chore boy were in there greasing boots and otherwise making themselves presentable for the burials that were to take place later in the day.

Jack nodded without speaking, then slowly pointed first to one wall bunk, then to a second one. With the chore boy watching from perfectly round eyes, Frank went over and took down the war bags that were suspended from both bunks. He upended them onto the bunks and pawed through the private effects of Carter, Beasely, and Billings, looking for letters with return addresses on the envelopes or beneath the signatures of those who had written the letters. But in neither case was there a single letter.

There were razors, soap, odds and ends of personal importance to the men who had lived out of those war bags, but nothing that would allow Frank to identify any next of kin.

He put everything back into both bags, straightened up, shoving his hat back, and turned. "Jack, did you ever hear either of them mention family or folks, such-like?"

Brady shook his head. "No. I don't recollect either Gus nor Dusty talkin' about their personal lives. Nor Howard either, for that matter, but then he likely wouldn't have mentioned those things to us fellers in the bunkhouse. Maybe, over at the main house, there might be something. . . ."

Frank took the war bags, the booted carbines that had belonged to the pair of dead rangemen, went back to the hitch-rack in front of the barn, and lashed them to his saddle under the solemn gaze of those two men inside the barn. Then he struck out for the main house. Evidently Helen Hill had seen him coming, because just as he started up the low, broad steps to the porch, she appeared.

Frank nodded, removed his hat, and studied her for a moment before speaking. She looked pale, and there was no way of telling from looking at her now that she had ever smiled, had ever shown friendliness. He hoped her dead-level gaze at him was occasioned by anything except his presence in the yard yesterday, which had precipitated the two killings, but he doubted that it did. She stood at ease, but the expressionless way she was regarding him seemed absolutely and dispassionately cold.

"Mrs. Hill, I had to pick up the personal things Carter and Billings had at your bunkhouse," said Hadley.

She nodded. "I saw you do that, Constable."

"Well . . . and to ask if maybe there might be something among Mr. Small's papers that'd give me an idea about who to notify."

"There was nothing at the bunkhouse?" she asked quietly, her voice not hostile but perfectly flat.

"No ma'am. I'd like to know about Howard Beasely, too." When she simply stood there gazing at him Frank decided to give it up. He offered a faint smile as he said, "Well, it doesn't have to be done today."

She ignored that. "Constable. Yesterday when you were in the parlor with my brother, I was in the kitchen. I didn't intentionally eavesdrop, but you were not trying to hold your voice down."

Frank understood. "And you heard."

"Yes. Do you truly believe Chet would have authorized that lynching?"

He did in fact believe that her brother would have authorized the lynching of horse thieves; he knew from lifelong experience that many big ranchers not only authorized their riders to lynch rustlers and horse thieves, but also participated in such matters themselves. But what she had asked was not what he was thinking about, so he offered an ambiguous reply.

"Mrs. Hill, it's been done out here hundreds of times. It's been range law since I was a boy. Horse thieves, murderers, cattle rustlers. I don't believe anyone will ever find all the secret graves." He shifted the hat in his hands and regarded its sweat-stained crown. "There was no other law in those days, Mrs. Hill. I've lived alongside it, and so have a great many other people. But that man your brother's rangemen hanged was not a horse thief." Frank's eyes swept up to her face. "I'll tell you the same thing I told that lynched man's brother last night. It was murder. It was also a lousy, rotten, senseless thing to do. At least they should have first proved that feller was a horse thief, which they couldn't have done. Mrs. Hill, we can stand out here talkin' all day, and what we'll end up sayin' is that it was a mistake. A damned awful mistake. And five men are dead because of it." He raised the hat to his head. "I don't think either of us will ever live through another tragedy like that one, and I'm sorry about what happened to your brother. I don't believe it was my fault—but I guess if I hadn't come out here yesterday, it wouldn't have happened."

He stood looking down into her expressionless face with its pale golden complexion and large, perfectly motionless eyes. "Well...."

She moved slightly, shifting her weight. "I don't want to blame you," she said in a deeper voice. "I don't want to blame anyone. I don't know enough about all that happened to place blame or to make judgments.... The wagon came back over an hour ago." She tipped her face to glance at the position of the sun. "I think I would appreciate it if you could stay for the funerals." Her lovely eyes came down to his rugged features. "Or isn't that proper out here, you having been involved?"

He smiled at her. "I'd be right honored to stay, and it's done out here like I guess it's probably done everywhere else. When a man dies, he don't have any enemies, Mrs. Hill."

She leaned slightly until her back and shoulders touched the closed door behind her. Without looking at him, she said, "I've been out here a month. Aside from Howard Beasely and my brother, and two or three of the riders who have been very nice to me, I don't know anyone. Constable Hadley, I need someone."

He was not as prepared for her candor as he probably should have been, but then he did not know her very well. Instinct prompted his reply to her. "I'll do anything I can do, Mrs. Hill." Remembering what Jack Brady had confided to him in town, he also said, "You've got to have a range boss to replace Howard. And you've got to have rangemen to replace the others. If you'd like I'll look around town and see what I can turn up. Right now there's mostly just riding and sort of minding things to be done, but directly it'll be time to gather, cull and sort, and make up the drive to rails' end. That'll come in the autumn, so you have a couple of months yet, but you'd ought to have things ready by then."

She nodded her head a little absently and looked down across the subdued, empty yard. "I don't know anything about those things. And I know the men want to leave." She faced him. "Everything came at once, Constable."

He saw the stricken look behind the oncoming tears and moved to alleviate both, if he could. "You got your share all at once for a fact, but instead of worryin' yourself skinny, start planning. I'll start finding men for you first thing in the morning. This time of the riding season, they aren't as common as they usually are, but we'll find them." He held her gaze. "About the ranch, quit fretting. There are plenty of folks in the Copperdust Hills country who'll pitch in and help you. About the other . . . let it lie, Mrs. Hill. Just do what you got to do and let it lie, and maybe in a few months, or maybe a year or so, we can sit down and talk it all out. But you're not goin' to have the time to fret about that, too, for the next few months."

She nodded up at him. "Constable Hadley, I'll be forever grateful."

Embarrassed, he nodded as he turned to go back down across the yard. "I'll go brush off," he told her, and went down to the bunkhouse where even the cook was digging in his sack for presentable attire. The three rangemen were in the room along with the cook and chore boy. Frank tossed his hat onto the long table near the stove and said, "Who wants to quit?"

All five of them stopped moving and looked around.

He said it again. "Who wants to quit? No reason why you shouldn't. Mr. Small's dead, the range boss is dead. Carter and Billings are dead, too. There's nothin' to hold the outfit together except you fellers. Hell, I can't think of a better reason for quitting. There's just a lady up at the main house who don't know up from down about runnin' a big cow outfit." He ignored their expressionless faces and went to the stove to shake the coffeepot. It was empty. He said, "Hell, any one of you could find another riding job within a hundred miles of here without any trouble." Finally he slowly turned to face them. "You want to know what I think? Any son of a bitch who'd quit an outfit under these circumstances—I wouldn't spit on his belly if his guts was on fire!"

Frank walked out through the back door to the wash rack, tucked his collar under, pushed up his sleeves, and filled the basin with water to scrub with. There was not a sound behind him through the open door inside the bunkhouse until he was toweling off. Then the whiskery-faced cook stepped into the opening and glared.

"Who in the hell said I was quitting?"

Frank lowered the towel. "No one."

"Then how's come you to come in here and just because you're wearin' that damned badge think you can insult folks?"

Frank showed a perfectly bland expression. "I didn't insult anyone, friend."

"The hell you didn't!"

Frank finished toweling off, then smiled at the stiffly irate older man. "Mister, what I said was, anyone who would quit under these circumstances. . . . But hell, friend, you just told me you weren't goin' to quit. I admire you; it's just those that figure to quit I was talkin' about. Not you, friend."

The cook stood bristling, but in the face of Frank Hadley's warm smile he could not hold that mood very long, so he turned and stamped back to finish getting ready for the funeral.

There was no conversation in the bunkhouse as the men went back to brushing and polishing, but when Frank walked back inside to borrow a horse brush to clean his hat with, a red-necked, horse-faced, blue-eyed tall cowboy puckered up and began to whistle.

The cook disappeared, was gone almost thirty minutes and returned freshly shaved, his cheeks slightly inflamed from the uncommon scraping they had had, and when that red-necked rangeman turned to look at him, the cook raised a stiff finger. "Henry, if you make one damned smart remark, the whole lot of you'll get goat stew for the rest of the month. Just one damned smart remark!"

Not a word was said, but the red-necked cowboy looked around, rolled up his eyes, and went back to fingering axle grease onto his boots.

Jack Brady dug in the very bottom of his possible sack, then straightened up with a bottle of whiskey. Everyone stopped to look. Brady put the bottle on the table, then shrugged and walked away. One at a time they filed over, took a couple of pulls, and went back to work. Only when the chore boy, who was perhaps seventeen years old but small enough to look three or four years younger, sidled up as the others had done, did anyone look disapproving. A dark, swarthy cowboy with high, flat cheekbones and a hooked nose scowled. He did not say a word; he simply scowled. But such was the effect when that hawklike nose and those very dark eyes showed displeasure that the chore boy sidled right on past.

Small Ranch was not only very large and successful; it had also been established for many years, and during the course of all that time, the range-cattle business being what it was, there had been casualties. The cemetery was enclosed in a wrought-iron fence to keep cattle out, and stood upon a slight, broad knoll about a half mile from the yard.

There were several large trees out there. There were also tracks leading from the yard to the knoll, but they were discernible only to someone walking that distance.

The wagon was already out there, four corpses shrouded in clean canvas lying stiffly on the straw-strewn bed with no way of telling one from the other except that initials had been painted in black across the upper half of each bundle.

Frank had thought the ranch would have buried its men in pine boxes as they did in town. There was a journeyman carpenter in Blythe who turned out fine pine coffins.

Frank had also expected that there would be a minister out there from town. Instead, the freshly shaven cocinero stepped forth to say one prayer over all four dead men. When he pulled a dog-eared Bible from a sagging coat pocket, a white handkerchief came partway out with the book and remained hanging half-exposed as he began to read.

Surprisingly, the cook had a strong, deep, resonant voice. And he read well. Frank stood bare-headed with the others, alternately watching the cook and Helen Hill. She was impassive in her black attire. He thought irreverently that she was an uncommonly pretty woman.

The cocinero finished praying, closed his Bible, and shoved it and the handkerchief back into his coat pocket, then gave an inpromptu eulogy over each of the men as the range riders lowered them into the earth. Again Frank Hadley was surprised; the cook did a professional job with each eulogy, did not stumble over a single word, did not pause to grope for things to say. Frank was so intrigued by the cook's expert delivery that he forgot to watch Helen Hill.

Then it was over.

Jack Brady and another rangeman remained behind to shed their coats, put their hats aside, take hold of the shovels, and begin filling the graves. Frank, walking slowly back, put on his hat and looked to his right. Helen Hill was walking beside him, her head slightly to one side and slightly downward. They returned to the yard without speaking.

She stopped when the chore boy, the cook, and a rider turned away, waited a moment and then looked up at Frank as she spoke. "I was thinking of something you said on the porch, Mr. Hadley. . . . Dead men don't have enemies. Isn't that another way of saying we should speak no evil of the dead?"

He hadn't thought of it like that, but he was willing to. "Maybe. I suppose if we could do that, it would be best, Mrs. Hill."

"Can't we, Constable?"

He met her steady gaze and nodded very slowly. "I guess we can."

"Then I don't suppose you and I will ever have that private talk, will we?"

He returned her look with a steady gaze of admiration. She was wise, he thought. She could not know, but she surely suspected, that he knew things about all those men they had buried this afternoon; what she was doing now was conveying to Frank Hadley that whatever he knew, she did not want to know.

He smiled softly at her. "I guess not. I'll see you to the house." Midway across the yard, when she glanced around, he said, "I'll find men for you. As for the rest of it—it's not like back east, so if you decide in a while you don't like it out here, I'll introduce you to some of your neighbors who would be pleased to own a piece of Small Ranch."

At the porch steps she faced him again. "I like it. I've always liked it. I've visited out here before, years ago. Constable . . . ?"

He headed her off this time. He did not like people to thank him. "I've got to get back. In a day or two I'll ride back out here. Meanwhile, those fellers in the bunkhouse will stay, so what you've got to do is start thinking ahead." He nodded, turned, and went back to his horse, untied, snugged up the cincha, stepped across the saddle, and rode out of the yard on his way back to Blythe. He had intended to compliment the cranky ranch cook, but because he was trying to imagine where he was going to turn up a range boss and three good rangemen this late in the season, he completely forgot about the cook.

By the time he drifted into the back alley on the east side of town and dismounted to lead his horse into the livery barn, it was dark and the café was closed. While there were a few lights showing around town, most of them—except for Bud Arlo's saloon—shone from the windows of residences.

At the jailhouse he went inside briefly before locking up and heading on a diagonal course for the saloon. As before when he had walked in on a weekday night, while Bud's place had a few customers, it was quiet; townsmen, who had the advantage of walking across the road to have a drink or a game of cards any time they wished to, did not enter a saloon with the pent-up exuberance of rangemen.

Bud brought a glass of beer, set it up, and raised an eyebrow. "You cleaned your hat. Is someone gettin' married, Frank?"

Hadley lifted the glass, looked down his nose at Bud Arlo, and drank deeply, then set the glass down and said, "No. They buried Chet Small this afternoon. Him and those three riders of his."

Bud did not pursue the subject.

"And," stated Frank, "they need three more riders to round out the crew."

Bud's expression brightened. "There were three fellers in here this afternoon lookin' for work."

"What did they look like, Bud?"

Arlo leaned down and screwed up his face. "Like they

know the work. Older fellers, about my age; not as old as you, Frank. They're bedding in the loft at the livery barn, if you want to talk to them."

Frank finished the beer and snorted. "As old as you are, but not as old as I am—thanks, Bud. I appreciate compliments."

CHAPTER 15

The Last Shot

JASPER Tobin was out in front of the café the following morning when Constable Hadley came across the road on his way from the rooming house to the café. He scowled at the sight of the paunchy liveryman. Frank was not a testy man but, like many people, he skirted close to it first thing in the morning before he'd had his coffee, and right now he was remembering Jasper's nosiness the previous morning.

He nodded and would have pushed past, but Jasper stopped him. "I figured you might want to know, Frank. That feller who shot Gus Carter hired a rig and went drivin' north, like he did just before he shot Carter."

Frank studied the coarse features in front of him. "By any chance did he have a shovel along this time, too?"

Jasper shook his head. "No, but he taken something fair-sized and all wrapped in gunnysacks."

Frank squinted around at the early sunlight to estimate the time. Then he asked how long ago Mark Forrest had left town in the rented rig, and Jasper made a little fluttery hand gesture. "I'd say maybe an hour. No more'n that. It wasn't quite breaking day."

"Well hell," grumbled the lawman, and sighed. "All right, Jasper. Go down and rig out my horse, and tie it in the alley. I'll be along as soon as I've eaten breakfast."

He stood a moment watching the liveryman depart, trying to imagine what Mark Forrest was up to now—and getting more irritable by the minute. He was sure he knew where Forrest had gone—up to that grave in the foothills—but why? Forrest knew who was buried up there. Maybe to exhume the remains and put them into a box or a trunk, or whatever it was he had taken up there with him in the buggy.

Frank entered the café and grunted like a sullen boar-bear at the first man who greeted him and went to the counter. When the disagreeable café man arrived for his order, Frank said, "Eggs this morning, and turn 'em over and fry 'em until there's nothing left to jiggle. You understand what I mean?"

The café man was also one of those individuals who was not happy first thing in the morning. "You got any idea how many million gawddamned eggs I've fried in my lifetime?" he snapped.

Frank sat back considering the café man and drumming on the countertop. He finally said, "No, I haven't. But so help me, if you fetch my breakfast eggs with one damned tiny wiggle in 'em, I'm coming over the top of this counter, tear off your fat arm, and beat your head in with it. Now git!"

The café man departed, several other diners turned mild looks of disapproval in Frank's direction, and if any of them had had some idea of striking up a conversation, that passage between Frank and the café man killed it.

The eggs arrived resembling a pair of deflated saddlebags and close to the same russet color. Frank ate them, drank coffee, and began to feel human. When the café man returned as Frank was rising to place coins beside his plate, Frank smiled, and the café man stood stone-still. After Frank had left the café, a bearded big burly freighter raised his eyes when the café man said, "That's the trouble with lawmen. You never know what danged mood they'll be in."

The freighter had what he thought was an answer. "Well, next time he comes up for election, get rid of him."

Two townsmen, both muscular men from the blacksmith shop, turned slowly to study the bearded man, and the cook's eyes flashed. "Get rid of him! Hadley's the best lawman this country ever seen. I been here twenty-three years; I've seen my share of the other ones. Not a one of 'em could hold a candle to Frank Hadley!"

The bearded freighter looked around, saw the looks he was getting, pulled his head down a little, and concentrated on his coffee without saying another word.

Outside, it was not as chilly as it ordinarily was about daybreak. Spring was past and summer was settling in, which meant that although the nights would remain cold for another month or so, the early mornings would be a little warmer. It also meant the days would be longer, which was what Frank Hadley was counting on as he left town on a northwesterly course; if the sun did not set very early tonight, he would be able to return to town before dark—providing something in the foothills did not delay him. In his line of work, Frank had learned long ago to make two estimates in a situation like this, one to cover what he would like to see happen and the other one to cover what Frank's inherent cynicism encouraged him to suspect probably would happen.

He did not get close to the foothills until the sun was high; there was brilliant summertime warmth over the entire valley, and he rolled up his old jacket and tied it behind the cantle.

He gave a cursory gaze along the foothills to the east and west. He did not expect to see anything and, except for a drift of settling dust, he did not see anything. He also studied the far mountainsides all the way up to the permanent ice fields. At the lower elevations there was a faint filminess where dust was settling. For lack of anything better to do, he traced out the course of that dust. It came down from the forest to the foothills, southward and a little to the east. He told himself it had probably been made by some Small Ranch riders combing the upper foothill country to turn back livestock, get them out of that cougar and bear country.

He rolled a smoke and reflected on the three range riders he had routed out of the hay last night down at the livery barn. He had sent them out to be hired by Mrs. Hill. He lit up, remembering how, even though the trio had clearly been badly in need of employment, they had hung fire when Frank had explained that they'd be working for a woman. Eventually they had agreed to ride out, but since Frank had felt their reluctance, he thought he might make a sashay past the ranch this afternoon on his way back to see if they had arrived, and if they had been hired. If they hadn't, he was going to have to start over again, and it was late in the season for finding worthwhile range riders.

Before he was within a couple of miles of that little knobby hill where the grave was, his horse had decided that what Frank wanted was to follow fresh wagon-tire tracks. The animal dropped his head and slogged along between the tracks on a loose rein.

Frank smashed out his smoke atop the saddlehorn and watched a distant bunch of cows with sassy-fat calves, and several does accompanied by a picture-book buck deer with a rack of horns that would send a trophy hunter to bed unable to sleep. The deer were closer; in fact, they were less than a mile away. They were not browsing, but were standing like statues looking over in the direction of that knobby little hill. Frank guessed what intrigued them; Mark Forrest was over there. But Frank was only partly correct.

When he passed around the sloping haunch of the flat topped, long land-swell that obstructed his view of the area around the little hill, he saw fresh shod-horse tracks in the grass. They were so fresh that even Frank, who was no sign reader, could make them out very clearly.

He reined to a halt and studied the tracks. They seemed to veer from the northeast in the direction of the rear of the little hill, crossing Mark Forrest's wagon-tire sign and passing from Frank's view on around toward the backside.

For no discernible reason, Frank had a bad feeling. He looked roundabout and still saw nothing but the cattle and deer, swung to the ground, tied his animal to a scraggly bush, yanked loose the tie-down over his six-gun, and started to carefully stalk ahead.

There was not a sound. There were not even any birds around. He got close to the haunch of the hill and listened. There was still not a sound, and that worried him. If Mark Forrest had begun his exhumation, or whatever it was he had come up here for, there should have been noise. Moving with great care, he palmed his Colt and inched around the sloping side of the hill. He halted when he caught sight of the buggy with its big stud-necked old Morgan mare dragging her lines with the check-rein unhitched, picking grass as contentedly as she could be. Then he heard a man's sharp, hard voice say, "You son of a bitch, you figured you could beat hell out of me an' I'd be scairt afterwards and leave the country! I been waiting. I knew you'd come back up here to the grave. I owe you for that beating. I always pay up on a debt, Forrest!"

Constable Hadley tried to place the voice but failed. He also tried to fit the fierce statement into what he knew, and he did not fail this time. Mark Forrest had beaten Howard Beasely and shot him. He had, he told Frank, caught another Small Ranch cowboy and beat him, too—and got the names of the men who had lynched Frank's brother. *That* was who had to be around there now—a vindictive, vengeance-haunted cowboy, one of the crew who had been at the lynching of Mark's brother, who clearly had not left the country as Jack Brady had thought, but had gone back into the mountains to keep his vigil against the day he could catch Mark Forrest. And this was the day.

A fresh voice spoke up, and Frank stopped breathing for a couple of seconds. It was a woman's voice. "Luther, it's over. Dusty is dead, my brother is dead. The man buried here—"

"You shut your damned mouth," snarled the rangeman. Then, in a voice congealed by bitter sarcasm, he went on. "I seen you ridin' up here this morning. I watched you, Miz' Hall. I used to watch you at the ranch. . . . I got somethin' in store for you, too. Damned rich easterners comin' out here—" The bitter voice suddenly changed pitch. "Forrest! You move again and I'll blow your guts out past your backbone!"

Helen Hill spoke again, and Frank Hadley could detect no hint of fear in her voice. "Luther! It's over. It's finished. Listen to me; there have been five men killed, over a terrible mistake."

Luther snarled his answer. "Lady, I don't give a damn about them. That son of a bitch standing there balancin' that headstone caught me unawares and give me a beating. That's what I'm goin' to settle up for. Now you keep your damned mouth shut!"

Frank had sweat running under his shirt. He gripped his Colt hard, studied the amount of ground he had to cover before he could see around there, and took two steps before Forrest's voice stopped him.

"Hadley'll be after you. You'll spend the rest of your life hiding and dodging. A beatin' isn't like a killing, Grant."

Frank remembered the man now. His name was Luther Grant, and he had been one of the riders with Small in the jailhouse office that day Small had tried to get Jack Brady to say Forrest had murdered Gus Carter. Frank did not remember much about Luther Grant, except that he was a hard-faced man, the color of dull bronze, lean and sinewy.

Frank took two more steps, wiped sweat off his gun palm, took a fresh grip, and took another two steps. Now he could see two dozing saddle horses, one of which clearly belonged to Luther Grant, which meant the other one had been ridden up here this morning by Helen Hill.

Frank leaned past some underbrush, very slowly, and saw Helen Hill and Mark Forrest. Mark had several gunnysacks lying at his feet where he had unwrapped a large headstone that he was balancing with one hand. Evidently Mrs. Hill had come up here this morning either by accident or by prearrangement, but in either case she had been helping Mark Forrest put the headstone in place above his brother's grave. Luther Grant, Frank knew now, had been responsible for the dust he had seen coming down from the forested slopes to this place.

Frank put a thick thumb atop the hammer of his Colt, made sure of his footing, and was about to take the final step ahead to face Luther Grant when Helen Hill spoke again.

"Luther, how much money is your beating worth? You don't look badly hurt. . . . Luther, let me pay you, and ride away."

The vengeful rangeman gave a hard, short laugh. "That son of a bitch ain't worth the price of it, Mrs. Hill. He ain't worth anything but a killing. Forrest!"

Frank took the last step and swung slightly to his left. He saw Luther Grant at roughly the same moment the three people saw him. He had their looks of pure astonishment fixed forever in his mind as he saw Luther Grant's belated reaction begin — Grant was curving his gun barrel in Frank's direction.

Frank hauled back the hammer and depressed the trigger. He did that twice. The gun's roar startled the horses so badly that they shied and flung half-around. From the side of his vision, Hadley saw Mark Forrest grab Helen Hill and drop down behind the gravestone with her. He also saw the orange mushroom of Luther Grant's muzzle blast as Frank was hauling back for his third shot. Then Grant's legs sprang loose and he fell forward on his stomach.

Frank shook off sweat, waited a moment for the gunsmoke to rise, and walked ahead, ignoring the man and woman standing up behind the headstone. He tipped Grant over with a boot toe, then sighed. His first bullet had missed Grant completely. The second one had made a curious injury; it had hit Grant on the side of the neck, had followed on around and finished its course with stunning impact at the base of Grant's skull. Then it had gone eastward out over the range.

Grant was gushing blood, but he was not dead. After kneeling to make an examination, Frank was satisfied he would not die if the flowing blood was stopped. He turned and said, "Mark, lend me a hand!"

They worked roughly, but rapidly and efficiently, until they had the blood staunched under shirt-tail and neckerchief bandages. Mark leaned back, eyeing Luther Grant. He did not speak; he simply wagged his head. Then he smiled wanly at Frank, and the lawman returned the smile. Mark said, "I'm right obliged, Constable."

Frank stood up and began reloading as he glanced over to where Helen Hill was standing beside the fallen gravestone. So that was what Forrest had loaded into the buggy in town this morning: a headstone. Hell, if he'd known that, he would not have come out here. He slammed the reloaded weapon into its holster and met Helen Hill's gaze. And if he had not come out here this morning, those two people would be dead now. At least Forrest would be, and he rather suspected that within a week or two Helen Hill's body would have been at the bottom of a canyon in the mountains somewhere, too.

He turned as Forrest picked up a six-gun from the grass at graveside, shook off dirt, and holstered it. Mark said, "You know who he was, Constable?"

Hadley answered shortly. "That range rider for Small you knocked the names of your brother's lynchers out of."

Forrest nodded and gazed at Helen Hill. She had not moved since before the shooting. She looked pale but resolute. Forrest said, "She rode out this morning to take some measurements, Constable. She was goin' to have one of those steel fences made at the shop on the ranch, then brought out here and put around my brother's grave."

Frank's composure was returning. He nodded gravely at the handsome woman. "That's a real decent thing to do."

She finally moved and walked over to them, keeping the unconscious man on the ground behind her. She had clearly witnessed a shooting and had been able to hold herself together, but probably had no intention of seeing how much of this sort of thing she could tolerate by looking at the bloody man in the grass behind her.

"Before Luther came up, Mr. Forrest. . . ."

"Yes'm?"

"I was asking, would you help me? Would you hire on at the ranch?"

Frank lifted his hat to mop sweat, then lowered it, gazing at Mark Forrest. He and the woman waited. Mark nodded, but only after a long moment, and when he replied to her, he offered no explanation for that delay. He simply said, "Yes'm."

Frank let go a big breath and looked out to where the horses were. "Mark, lend me a hand gettin' Grant tied to his horse, will you?"

A half hour later, with the sun on the wane, Frank

headed back for town, leading the horse with his wounded prisoner atop it. Back where he had left Mark Forrest and Helen Hill, they were struggling to do what they had been engaged in before Luther Grant had come upon them — to balance that heavy gravestone so that it could be tamped into place.

Frank looked back once from a couple of miles out as he was looping his reins before rolling a smoke. It seemed that Mark Forrest and Helen Hill worked very well together.

Frank grunted, lit his smoke, glanced dispassionately at the dead weight on the horse he was leading, and wagged his head. There was an almost infinite variety of fools in this world, but a man who couldn't take a shellacking without turning so venomous he wanted to commit murder to even up for a beating was, in Frank's view, one of the biggest and least admirable fools of them all.